About Rishabh

RISHABH PURI is an entrepreneur of Indian origin with business in Nigeria, Dubai, and China. Despite his demanding day job, he finds time to indulge in his passion for writing fiction. He is a national bestselling author with three books penned under his name - 'Inside the Heart of Hope', 'Flying Without Wings', 'Seductive Affair' 'Aavya' and 'Forever Yours'. His readers have loved and enjoyed all his books immensely, and 'Every Kiss a Poem' is his sixth book.

His writings are mostly centred on the beauty of hope, love, and life. Rishabh is also an avid traveller and a supercar enthusiast. He is based in Lagos, Nigeria and Dubai UAE, but visits India regularly, returning to his birthplace, Chandigarh, which remains immensely close to his heart.

Every Kiss a Poem

Every
Kiss a
Poem

Rishabh Puri

KALAMOS LITERARY SERVICES LLP

Kalamos Literary Services LLP
Email: info@kalamos.co.in | editorial@kalamos.co.in

Published in 2020
by
Kalamos Literary Services

ISBN- 978-93-87780-30-9

Cover designed and typeset in Kalamos Literary Services LLP
Print and bound in India.

Acknowledgements

Love is the greatest certainty this life has to offer, but life happens where love's details get hazy. The love you want and think you deserve might not be the love that saves you in the end but looking back on a life of blessings I see now that at every turn, love was with me, in many forms, hand in hand.

I'd like first and foremost to thank God for the overwhelming blessings He has graced me with, being made from love and showing nothing but love to His whole creation. I would also like to thank my mother, father, and sister for their love and support throughout my whole life. This foundation of love and unconditional acceptance has been the firmest foundation I've ever known, and it allows me to fly.

The doctors who have, through their love of their art, taken on a case as difficult as mine and made it their own. Dr. Alok, my heart surgeon, my brother. My life has been in your hands so many times, and you have never shied away from the challenge of keeping me going. Dr. Dennis Lox, your seemingly boundless knowledge is matched only by the sense of humour that was able to lift my spirits from their lowest point. Without these doctors, I would not have had the life in my body to put pen to page. To Dr. Eliot Brinton, my gratitude for the years of study and expertise that led me to you is beyond what words can communicate. Your work has changed my life for the better. I am beyond grateful. And Dr. Dinesh Nair You take the time to listen and to make your patients feel valued and respected, treating others as you would want to be treated. I thank God often for you. Thank you for who you are.

Finally, I am grateful to you, my dearest reader, who loves words and loves stories about love. Whether this is the first of my books you've ever picked up or you are a devoted fan, you bring my dreams to life each day, and I hold you warmly in my heart. I hope you enjoy this book.

One

Vikram Shan came into work that day determined to ignore Ashok, no matter what else happened. His fists clenched as tight as his sealed resolve. Until 9:00 AM, Ashok was nothing more than a mosquito buzzing in his ear. But once Vikram swiped his key-card at the door and clocked in, he was an M.R. Enterprises employee. Ashok was no longer his annoying college buddy, but the head of sales for the Chandigarh office. He was also Vikram's boss.

Though Ashok was Vikram's boss, he had crossed a line. A line he had crossed many times before, but this time it was different. Ashok had woken up Sunday morning with hangover breath and Vikram's new girlfriend in his bed. Vikram was sure that Ashok must have had prepared an apology for Monday morning. After all, he had an entire day to do so. He would try to heal some of the pain he'd caused with a sheepish apology and a packet of crisps dropped on Vikram's desk.

However, Vikram was also sure that Ashok would apologize not due to any remorse or guilt, instead, he would do so for 'coffee'. No one else could make coffee quite the way that Vikram could. And Ashok had proved, while they were still in college, that he was willing to brave humiliation to get his caffeine fix.

But Ashok would have no such luck today. Vikram had come equipped with an industrial-sized mug of black tea for his own caffeine needs, and in no condition was he going to make a pot of coffee for Ashok. He was prepared to use it to keep himself alert while poring over the sales reports he'd created yesterday – he felt it was better to work on a Sunday then to dwell on the fact that Ashok took away another woman from him. These reports should give him an hour in which he could pretend to be too busy to help his boss. Without the coffee pot filled, Vikram hoped Ashok would have a headache by lunchtime.

Vikram ignored his ringing phone and flicked through his emails without the intention of reading them at the moment. It was going to be a busy day. Sahana Bhat, from the New Delhi marketing office, had moved into the Chandigarh office last Friday. She was already hoping to schedule a meeting with Ashok for this morning. Vikram ignored her email as well as the obnoxious ecard that Ashok had sent him. He wasn't sure that they made e-cards reading, 'Sorry not sorry I slept with another one of your girlfriends. I'm a jerk, and I have to prove my macho-superiority to you in all aspects of my life.'

He pulled his notebook from his briefcase. There was no way to handle this besides writing it out. Vikram was a writer out of necessity. There was no other tool he'd found that allowed his life to make sense. If processed through the lens of poetry, his irritation would either dissipate enough to let him get on with his life or narrow down his focus until it was so sharp he could use it to scalp Ashok.

You were a masterpiece. All I wanted was to stand before you and watch, admiring the way color moved through you. You were bold and glittering, lush with beauty and a mind whose thoughts I only dreamed of occupying. I could have lost myself in the details God gave you when he bent low to sprinkle cinnamon freckles on your shoulders like a night sky full of warm stars. I could have written poetry connecting each moment like a constellation until it spelled out your name. I was content to love and let you shine.

Then came an art thief with clumsy fingers and a smile like the bleeding edge of a silver blade. He slipped a dagger into the edge of your canvas and tore you away, spiriting you off. A thief in the night, an adventure you had not taken yet, you folded into him easily, gone in the blink of an eye. Though he would not love your ragged edges as I would, though he would try to cram you into a frame you could not occupy. I was left staring at a blank wall, trying to make sense of this mess left behind. Alone, the observer. With nothing more to see. Me and only me.

It was a free write, and to many, it won't make sense, but Vikram felt good just to get it down. The rage flowing through him hadn't lessened any, but it felt cleaner. He understood his feelings more than he would have otherwise. He smirked as he closed the notebook, cracking his knuckles. It was time to get to work.

The early-birds to the office shot him looks of trepidation and concern as he settled in for the morning. He ignored them. Word on what Ashok had done had gotten around already. It was likely that Ashok had prepared his whole team. Vikram could imagine the email blast. *Once again, my completely unprofessional boundaries with my drinking buddy, I mean, my assistant, will be making your life difficult. Prepare accordingly.*

The problem wasn't just that Ashok had slept with his girlfriend, the bigger problem was it wasn't the first time that he had done so. And if Vikram didn't do anything this time, it would happen again. Ashok slept with anyone's girlfriend, but it didn't make it hurt any less. Also, Vikram had liked Pridima. She was pretty and an excellent dancer, she was detail-oriented and had a peculiar habit of doodling on every scrap of paper she could find.

Vikram was on his fifth date with her, and he was very excited about it. They were having a good time, or at least he thought so. He had left her drawing on a bar napkin for a moment to go to the bathroom. In the time before he returned, somehow, that bar napkin had found its way to Ashok's pocket with her number scribbled on it. The next day when Vikram had woken up alone to a text message that said, *we're not working out. sry. xx,* he'd already known who to blame before Ashok called.

Yes, she cheated, but he wasn't even mad at her. He was mad at Ashok. He wanted it to stop.

Vikram didn't even look up when a family-sized bag of crisps, a tin of cookies, and a to-go cup of coffee found themselves on his desk. Ashok had already prepared artillery to defend himself against Vikram's silent siege. The problem with having lived with Ashok for three years in college was that his boss knew Vikram's preferences. And he exploited them.

But Vikram wasn't giving in. Ashok couldn't buy his forgiveness by sending him a veritable breakfast feast. This time, he was not giving in. He chewed his pen and stared at his computer screen while Ashok greeted him, pleaded at him, and mocked him. He swatted the paper clip that Ashok tried to poke him with, rolling his eyes when his boss commanded him to speak.

"What do you want me to *say?*" Ashok asked, trying to keep the laugh out of his voice. "I saved you from that one. She was quite boring in bed and obviously bored with you. She wasn't worth your time, buddy--"

"She might not have been so boring if you had an emotional connection. If you had any passion for women you conquer and discard," Vikram bit out. He hadn't meant to surrender to speaking, but he could feel rage in his stomach burning him through like a hot coal.

"I don't believe the girl had that much passion for you to begin with if she went with me so fast," Ashok mocked. "Honestly, she wasn't that great in bed."

"I don't see why you keep doing this if you're not even happy with what you get from it," Vikram muttered. He clicked from spreadsheet to spreadsheet, acting like he was too busy to keep talking. Ashok spread his hands in supplication.

"I don't know what you want me to say," he said again.

Every time Ashok pulled something like this, Vikram hated him a little more. He knew Ashok had issues with commitment, and that he simply doesn't want to settle down. Hence, he kept on sleeping with random girls. Maybe by doing so, Ashok was able to convince himself he wasn't growing older. Vikram was under no such illusions about his own life. Haunting bar after bar in hopes of finding someone to love for the night sounded like a nightmare. He wanted to settle down, to find a wife, and spend his weekends reading poetry snuggled up on the couch next to her. He couldn't do that with Ashok under his feet all the time, tripping him up.

"I want you to say you're going to stop this," Vikram finally met Ashok's eyes, and the look of smug amusement evaporated from Ashok's face. "I want you to say you're going to grow up and stop this nonsense. It's exhausting. We're not kids anymore. This isn't college where you are messing around and your playboy antics are consequence free!"

But Ashok's customary smirk returned to his face at that, all wicked youth and mischief. Vikram was too tired for it. He clicked around on his spreadsheet, trying to lose himself in the comforting rhythm of statistics. He expected Ashok to say something in his own defense. Instead, his boss rapped his knuckles on Vikram's desk and headed towards his own office. As Ashok closed the door behind him, a hush fell over the bullpen where the sales team worked. It was broken only by the clatter of fingers on a keyboard, the sound of a printer running, a phone ringing somewhere down the hall.

"Get back to work," Vikram sighed after a moment. "We've got a busy day today."

Some of the workers grunted their agreement and turned to their desks. Headphones popped out of bags, coffee swilled and breakfast eaten, crumbs scattered across desks. The sales team braced themselves for another morning back at the office after a full weekend spent enjoying their homes and families. It was a grim reality. It was another Monday.

Vikram wished he could be one of them. He wished he was someone who didn't look forward to Mondays. He wanted a life outside of work filled with more interesting things than just the nine to five rhythm. But as he resumed his morning routine of spreadsheets and emails, he couldn't deny that he felt a strange happiness. This was as exciting as his life got. How sad was that?

The true highlight of his life drew nearer as the clock ticked closer to the lunch break. The many treats Ashok had left him as a peace offering sat untouched on his desk. It is during this lunch break when he could sit at his desk with a container of last night's leftovers, reading for an uninterrupted half hour. Today he'd spend it buried in the works of Rabindra Nath Tagore. He loved poetry. It was all dreamy mysticism and beauty. It drew him away from the dreary gray cubicles that he haunted in his waking days.

Of course, as the time grew close, his phone rang, and the familiar number flashing across the caller ID indicated that Ashok was calling. If it hadn't, though, Vikram still would have known who was calling. Ashok was standing in the doorway of his office, motioning for Vikram to join him inside. Vikram picked up the phone and hung up. Ashok rolled his eyes and ducked back into his office, presumably to call Vikram again. Vikram refused to give him the chance.

Sighing and shaking his sleeping leg awake, he ducked through the doorway of Ashok's office, a frown on his face.

Ashok's office was as dazzling and superficial as the man himself. All sleek, contemporary furniture imported from places where it snowed through spring, where people took coffee breaks in the middle of their day and refused to work in August. Neither Vikram nor Ashok worked like Europeans. They gave the Japanese a run for their money, devoting themselves to sleepless nights to make sure their clients were satisfied. But the looks of this office gave off the air of a nepotistic playboy who'd never done more than a day's work in his life. That was the impression Ashok loved to give every one of himself, fancy and carefree. The worried frown on his face was an unguarded expression that few people saw. Vikram was one of the lucky few.

"I am sorry," Ashok said, and Vikram could hear in his voice that this time he meant it. Vikram softened immediately in spite of himself. He was still angry, but he could feel his resolve waver. "I saw her eyeing up the bartender. I thought, you know, better a friend from whom you expect it than this girl betraying you with a stranger. She wasn't right for you, Vik. She's not the kind of woman you're looking for."

"I suppose she was the kind of woman you were looking for," Vikram snapped, but there was very little heat left in his reply. He thought of the chips on his desk and felt a little rotten. Ashok had a bizarre way of caring for his friends. If he were to try and view it through Ashok's warped sense of virtue, Vikram could see that his friend thought he was doing the right thing. If he found some company for the night in the process? All the better for him.

8

"A gold-digger with brains in her head but no heart inside her chest?" Ashok smirked, "nice for a night, but not even I am that shallow. I don't only care for what's on her chest-- I care for the sweetness of the heart inside of it." Vikram laughed, but Ashok continued. "And any girl who could give up a guy like you isn't a girl worth your time, buddy. It's why I test them for you. A girl who's true won't treat you that way. And you deserve a girl who's true."

Vikram sighed, relaxing into the chair in front of Ashok's desk. There was a picture of them at the beach in their last year of college, pulling silly faces. They were kids then. But now they were grown up, and the games they played were getting more and more dangerous by the minute.

"I'm running out of time to find a good girl who isn't married," Vikram sighed. "I want to marry for love. Is that unrealistic?"

"My parents would say yes," Ashok agreed. "Even I, in my more cynical moments, would call you a foolish dreamer. But that's who you are, Vikram. A man with a heart full of hope and a dream that never dies-- you're the kind of man a true girl could fall in love with."

"But she never will if you keep interfering!" Vikram blurted out. "With your cheesy smiles, flashing your Rolex and your limitless credit card around a bar. You enchant every girl with her sights set on greatness, or at least a great amount of money."

"Look," Ashok said. "If you're meant to fall in love, the right girl won't even notice me when you walk into the room. She'll choose you over me any day. It'll be how it is. Aren't you the great believer in poems and destiny?"

Vikram nodded. This was his one fault for which Ashok had teased him since forever. And it to this fault that Ashok had confessed that he was jealous of Vikram. Where Vikram was a dreamer, Ashok was a planner. And he planned meticulously, without the support of hope. To him, there was only realism and analysis of what could be gained or lost from an action. It was the reason he was good at what he did, good at pulling easy girls and hard deals.

"Your problem, Vik, is that you're too busy doubting yourself to chase your own dreams. It's what that girl, what was her name, Padma?"

"Pridima," Vikram corrected. Her name tasted sour in his mouth. He was already trying to forget her.

"It's what she said about you. Sometimes she would catch you thinking about kissing her, but you'd stop because you didn't think you were worthy of it. At first, she thought it was sweet. Then she found it annoying."

"Well, I'm annoying then," Vikram sighed. "What do I do about it?"

"Get brave, man," Ashok said. "Stand up to me for once. The next girl you fall in love with, I'll try as hard to take. But if you want her, if she's meant for you, then it's not going to work, is it? No matter how charming I am."

Vikram rolled his eyes. "Quit kidding." But he could see that Ashok, crazy as he was, was serious.

Ashok rapped his empty coffee cup on his desk in a gesture that was as pleading as it was direct. "Take your lunch break and think on it," he countered, pointing a convicting finger at Vikram. Vikram remained unconvinced. "In all your wishful thinking she'll come to you, and we can end this game once and for all. But I won't make it easy on you."

"You never do," Vikram wanted to sound stern, but he couldn't help but laugh. Ashok was crazy, but he did care. It was why he'd gotten Vikram this job in the first place. He'd helped a friend, i.e. Vikram, whose father had died, with a position and a place to stay until he could get his head on straight. It was why he was kind to Vikram's mother, even if he placed no value whatsoever on any woman Vikram tried to date. Ashok was an odd friend and maybe an awful person, but after all these years he was still trying to be Vikram's friend. That sort of loyalty was hard to come by.

Vikram was still contemplating Ashok's words when, on his way down to the cafeteria, he missed the first step at the top of the stairs. And from there, it was a long, painful way down to a hard landing.

Two

The worst part of falling down the stairs was the sound of everyone else cringing when he hit the ground. At least, that's what Vikram thought, a second before the pain blossomed across his head. Then he remembered that real pain was the worst sort of pain there was. Embarrassment sharpened the sting like salt in the wound.

As Vikram opened his eyes, trying to resist the searing pain across his body, he saw people gathered around him. It seemed the entire office had assembled at the bottom of the stairs in the five-seconds in which he fell down. Some were giving him a pitying look, and some were smirking. The humiliation of the fall just magnified the humiliation of the past weekend. Vikram was ready to be absorbed into the ground or to die from the injuries he'd sustained falling. Unfortunately, he wasn't going to die of anything other than shame, and shame seemed to be a slow-acting poison.

There was a whistle and a slow clap from the top of the stairs that Vikram recognized as Ashok. He forgot any good feelings he'd allowed himself to feel for his old friend. No, Ashok was the worst person alive. Anything Ashok did that seemed kind had all the sugar of a pit viper's venom in it. He laughed at his friends' misfortune so often that causing it was another source of weekend entertainment to him.

"I hate you," Vikram muttered into the stairwell tile. A throat cleared above him, closer than Ashok's manic laughter.

"Sir?" the voice asked. It belonged to a woman, melodic and bright as sunshine. It reminded him of bird-song. Not just the cartoon variety that orbited a person's head when they were concussed. Which, come to think of it, he might be. He'd hit his head pretty hard on his way down.

"Not you," he groaned, still into the tile. He could see a stiletto pump attached to a thin ankle, fashionable and polished. They couldn't have belonged to an intern. More of a regional manager type. He wasn't thinking clearly. He was--

"You're bleeding," she informed. Ah, that's what the sticky feeling around his eyes was. Vikram struggled to his elbows. His head gave a massive jolt of pain as he moved.

"I'm not sure you should move," she added. "Maybe someone should call the paramedics?"

"I hardly think it's that serious--" Ashok said from the top of the stairs.

"Obviously, the head of the sales department doesn't think of anything as 'that serious,'" the woman snapped, "Except fashion and posturing. I'm assuming by the line of your suit that you're Ashok Prasad?"

13

"That's half of what sales is, fashion and posturing. You chose an interesting detail to pick up on," Ashok observed, tapping his pen to his chest. Vikram wished that ink would get all over his friend's shirt. "But yes, I am he. I suppose, judging by the tone of your voice, you've already been listening to office rumors?"

"Rumors are half of marketing," the woman said. Her tone was patient, but something in it belied the irritation she was feeling. Ashok was joking. She was past that. "Something you should already know, of course. Something I might have been able to tell you earlier if you hadn't wasted my morning ignoring my emails."

The fire in the woman's voice was warm as it was bright. It was so alluring, Vikram thought it was making him as dizzy as the head wound he'd received. He might be in love, or he might be a moment away from passing out. He couldn't decide. The pulsing pain in his forehead throbbed like his heart.

"Ignoring-- ah," Ashok ran a hand through his carefully styled hair, trying to look sheepish. "My apologies, you must be Miss Sahana Bhat. I assure you, if I'd known you were this pretty, I wouldn't have let my assistant-- who is lying there crumpled at your feet-- put off our meeting for one second."

"Sexual harassment is a fireable offense," Sahana shot back. She didn't seem too ruffled by Ashok's attention. It was something she was used to dealing with in her line of work. She was professional and unflappable. Vikram knew Ashok well enough to see that under his calm exterior, this felt like a direct challenge to him. Ashok was envisioning a meeting of the minds, passionate arguments leading to passionate desk sex. Vikram felt offended on Sahana's behalf.

"Tell that to the loser looking up your skirt," Ashok countered. Sahana looked down closer at Vikram, who realized that no, it wasn't the head injury confusing him. He was a little bit in love with her. She narrowed her eyes at him, considering him as though she wasn't sure whether to help him up or kick him.

"The poor man is concussed," she said softly, finally deciding he was harmless.

"And bleeding all over your shoes," Ashok added. Sahana took a step back at that. Vikram thought he felt a little colder. But maybe that was blood loss.

"Can you stand?" she asked Vikram brisk. He found that at her urging, he could stand, blinking at her as he struggled to his feet. She examined him on his jaw, studying him for life-threatening injuries, no doubt.

"You'll live," she whispered to him with a conspiratorial smile. "But I don't blame you for wanting to avoid another day's work with that jerk." Vikram smiled with her. She then added a little loudly, "I imagine you'll need to take the rest of the day to go home and rest. Maybe get it checked out at the clinic if you experience any nausea or memory loss."

"Okay," Vikram agreed. He wasn't sure she had the authority to make him leave. But there was a note of pure steel in her voice that made it hard to disobey. She'd earned her position as head of marketing through grit and determination, not just by being a pretty face.

However, he didn't want to leave. The best part of his day had been meeting her. Now she was sending him off to fend for himself when he was injured and maybe near death. Well, he didn't think he was actually near death. But if it would get her to spend a moment longer in his presence, he might be able to fake it.

"Excuse me," she called to him, "you may want to take the elevator back up."

"It's only a half-flight of stairs," Ashok snapped, "he bumped his head, not broke his leg." Sahana turned to look at Ashok with a fire in her eyes that made Vikram feel dizzy again. He must be injured, he thought. Maybe Sahana was right to send him home. It was amazing that someone so young and pretty could have so much wisdom.

"You've worked him so hard that he's exhausted, and that's why he tripped in the first place." Sahana jabbed an accusatory finger in Ashok's direction. "If this is how you treat your staff--"

"So, am I a slacker who does no work? Or am I a slave driver who works my team so hard that they fall down the stairs to get a moment's reprieve from me?" Ashok replied sarcastically. Sahana looked murderous, but as Vikram brushed past Ashok on his way back to his desk, the other man's eyes lit up.

"That one," he whispered to Vikram. "That's the girl for you."

"Wha-what?" Vikram blustered, confused. How could a girl with that much passion and wit be the girl that Ashok found suitable for a quiet man like Vikram? She was a crackling hearth fire and he was a still cup of water. They couldn't mix. "I don't think--"

16

"You don't think highly of yourself enough, I know," Ashok said. "But that's the sort of girl with a fire in her heart and a beautiful face to boot. If she doesn't fall for false charms like mine, and I doubt she will, she could be the one."

"You're crazy," Vikram hissed, even as hope fluttered in his heart.

"I'll test her to see if she's true," Ashok continued. The impish grin on his face was no longer boyish and charming. Now it was immature, cunning and borderline evil.

"Don't do that!" Vikram snapped.

"Do what?" Sahana asked from behind them. If Vikram hadn't been on the solid ground of the office floor, he might have fallen over again. "Are you already trying to bully your poor beleaguered assistant into working? I've just told him that he could go home."

"With all due respect, ma'am, he's not your assistant to order around," Ashok replied. The wicked grin on his face showed that he wasn't irritated any longer. It was an exciting challenge for him now.

Sahana interrupted-- "with all due respect," and this time it was evident in her tone that she felt no respect was due.

But Ashok cut her off. "He's my assistant. Not yours. And since he is the person who schedules my meetings, he's the source of your frustrations this morning. So, I apologize for him for this rough start." Sahana looked infuriated, but she settled back on her heels and took a calming breath. Professionalism. She had it in spades. Vikram, who had never possessed that particular virtue, admired it in her.

"I accept your apology," she said, offering a graceful, manicured hand to Ashok, who took it.

"I agree, however, that Vikram should go home and get some rest. It's clear that after this weekend's antics, you need it." And with a devilish grin, Ashok cocked an eyebrow at Vikram. Vikram felt the hot coal of anger in his stomach growing again at Ashok's reminder. This was Ashok's way of insulting him further. It was neither a wise gesture nor was it kind. But Ashok did it anyway. It wasn't fair of Ashok to bring up something that he knew would only embarrass Vikram further, and Ashok knew it. However, he didn't care, and it was the worst aspect of him.

Vikram grumbled as he made his way back to his desk. Of course, now Sahana would think of him as a drunk as well as an incompetent. It was amazing how Ashok can leverage any situation – especially the one which he had worsened – and turn it to his own advantage.

Vikram wanted nothing more than returning to his home and read some good poetry to overcome his frustrations. He had a lot of leaves accumulated so far. He rarely vacationed, so he never felt the need to stay home idle. The worst part of working every waking second was that he didn't know what to do when he actually took a day off. However, given how Ashok had made his life miserable, maybe he should reciprocate. And the best way would be to do no work – especially when the company was going through a merger and the sales department, i.e. Ashok, needed him the most. Yes, it would be for the best. He'd take their advice and run with it. He would go home and do nothing but rest and read.

As Vikram started to leave, his thoughts diverted to Sahana, and the soft way she had looked at him, a smile playing on her full lips. She had bristled at Ashok's attentions.

Perhaps she found him as insincere as Vikram knew him to be. She was a smart woman. And it wasn't the only thing which Vikram found intriguing about her. He loved her manicured nails, the color of a tulip's deep red petals, the sheen of gold studs in her ears, the way her hair was pinned in a knot above her neck. She was professional, detailed, sharp with dark eyes that took in everything. But there was a softness, a sweetness in the collar of her shirt, the smooth way her clothes fit her body. She was lovely. Exquisite. A poem in a person. He wanted to read her, but they were at work. A million thoughts – romantic and such – were running through his mind as he stared at her on his way out. What would happen if he approached her? He was contemplating the answer, but it didn't matter because in that moment her eyes flicked up to meet his. She'd caught him staring. And she looked back.

"Vikram, is it?" she asked him. He nodded with a smile on his face, his fingers holding the place in his book as he shifted his briefcase in his other hand. A smile sparkled in her eyes when they met his. For a lightning moment, it was like they were the only two people in the world. "Nice book."

"Thanks," he said automatically. Then his mind caught up to him and he realized what she'd said. She was bright and funny, and she complimented a book of poetry that had changed his life. It had to be fate. It couldn't be a coincidence. He'd resigned himself to the fact that she was out of his league the second Ashok had come to him with his proposition. But looking at her, it was hard for Vikram to resist the thought that they might be good for each other.

Three

Sahana. Her voice, like a sunrise, like a musical note ringing clear as a bell in his head. Every time he conjured an image of her face in his mind, he couldn't help but smile. She was beautiful and bright-eyed. She was charming without trying. Many could try to imitate her, with years of training in elegance and poise, but only a few could truly do it. Sahana. Every detail of her stood gilded and glowing in his mind. Her lips like a flower, her voice like gentle rain, the fire of her heart bright enough to scorch anyone who dared to touch her.

To know her heart, he'd have to hold on through a trial that might blister his hands. But it was getting to know her that he craved most of all, even in its possible fatality. Even in its trials and struggles. In the end, he might not be good enough or pure enough to be with her. But Vikram could only dream, could only believe and try, in spite of all the differences: where she ruled, he served. Where she sparkled, he worked to reflect the light of others. In some ways, he was her inferior. But in other ways, they were compliments. Her sunlight to his shadow. Each let the

other seem more striking and fascin
they completed a puzzle.

These were the sorts of thir
reading on his afternoon off.

However, his pen to the page
bigger in his mind, like a magnify
easier to see its intricate details. T
tattoo on her elbow in irritation ev
way her gaze softened a little when ......med at Vikram. The
white of her teeth glinting in a smile that could swallow the
world. The deep curtain of her black hair. He wanted to pull
it around himself if he ever built up enough courage to lean
in and kiss her.

He had only met her three hours ago, and already, in his
mind, he'd revealed to her his most intimate secrets.
Something in his mind – more than intuition, more like fate –
seemed to know he could trust her with himself. When she
walked into a room, all eyes were on her. Men especially spent
so much time looking at her. It was easy to memorize the way
she moved, to watch her thoughts in her head before she
spoke them out loud. They'd be able to catch any tell or
falsehood in her body language the minute she tried to speak.

She was the kind of girl to whom you could write poems,
the sort of girl who inspired entire life works. She was a muse.
He wanted to live in the light of her inspiration for days on
end. Each touch of his pen to the page felt as though he had
dipped from a well of inspiration. He pursed his lips as he
scribbled into his notebook.

The curve of her
a cupid's b
from w
th

lips
w
...ich the moon hangs
...e twinkle in her eyes the light
from every star.
Our hearts beat in sync
our bodies magnetic.
She is the earth's surface and I
A meteorite
Gravity-drawn
Kiss crashing into her.

He stared at the page. He'd been writing since he was a child, but a poem that good had never come straight from his pen to the page. He was a writer who learned by revising, not the sort who lived in a world of pure art and stimulation. He was a crafter, a learner. He often had to play with structure, meditate on better words to use. But this felt like he'd reached into a river of inspiration and pulled it from the depths. Was it her sight that was still stuck in his mind? The thought of their first kiss? Or something more than that?

Perhaps it was only a mere coincidence. Shocked, he flipped a page and tried again.

She who was formed
to form words within me.
She who could pull a song
from a hollow heart of stone.
She who plays the river like a lire
strings the stars on her necklace.

Laugh heavy like a thunderstorm
pouring forth from full lips.
Goddess of the pen I hold close
opening the dry throat of my soul
into rapturous song once more.

His poems were a celebration, an easy flow of love and adoration. He hadn't recognized himself capable of until he'd done it. Not an exploration of the emptiness in his heart, but a quick jolt of joy broken down into short stanzas. How had someone warmed the cold in his heart, with a little bit of kindness and a lot of sharp, soulful attention?

Maybe that was why Ashok had agreed to Sahana's suggestion. Maybe that was why he'd smiled and allowed Vikram the time off. Behaving as though he were concerned that Vikram might be injured. He was trying to pass himself off as a hero, the considerate boss only looking out for his employee. Not to smooth over a rough morning or soothe Sahana's offended nerves. Instead, to keep Vikram away while Ashok began his conquest. Come to think of it, Ashok had seemed eager to see Vikram leave. He had shooed him out the door and push him back down the stairs to get him out of there. Maybe to get Sahana alone in his office.

The negative side of having a dream-possessed mind was it could conjure both good and bad images. And suddenly Vikram's mind reared to its ugly face. Vikram felt enraged. He sat on his couch staring at nothing, while in his mind's eye, the scene he was missing at work played out in his head. Once it started, he couldn't make it stop or distract himself from it.

He could only watch, the helpless onlooker in his own horrible imagination.

Ashok would close the door behind Sahana, smoothing his lapels. He'd crack another self-deprecating joke to see a glimpse of her sun-bright smile. He'd invite her to sit across from him and pour her a cup of tea, claiming the coffee machine was "broken" in Vikram's absence. If she accepted, he'd pull the tin of biscuits he kept and offer it to her. It would seem like he was sharing an inside joke about guilty pleasures instead of using a calculated move. Over tea and biscuits, they'd flirt, using the flimsy excuse that neither of them wanted to get down to business. In reality, they'd be like fighters in the ring, sizing each other up, each one deciding how much the other could take.

Then he'd touch her wrist to see if she'd draw her hand back and slap him. If she took it as a challenge, she'd advance, leaning in closer as he spoke. She'd slide one ankle against the other as an excuse to press her body towards him. It would allow him the intoxicating smell of her perfume that would encourage Ashok's interest. Then, she'd draw back, injuring his pride enough to inspire him to strike. Ashok was a cobra that way. If he was wounded, he'd strike back until he was either crushed or victorious. And Ashok was rarely crushed. He was the kind of man who found success under the most difficult circumstances.

From there, it wasn't hard to imagine Ashok's hand gripping her waist as he kissed her hard and possessive. He'd take what he thought he deserved. It wasn't hard to imagine Sahana surging to meet him kiss for kiss. She'd allow him to loosen her hair from its updo and letting it fall like a waterfall down her back. She was all fire and light, and Vikram knew what it would be like to press his mouth to hers.

It wasn't hard to imagine any of that, no matter how much it hurt Vikram to think of it. After all, wasn't that what Ashok had done with Vikram's last girlfriend? And the one before that? It was exactly what he'd threatened to do if Vikram didn't stop him once and for all.

But to stop him, Vikram would need to be brave. He would have to fight for what he wanted and show that he was the sort of man who deserved the sort of woman Sahana was.

The problem was that Vikram and Ashok had different expectations when it came to romance. Ashok was the kind of person who expected quick, fiery, ruinous passion. He wanted the sort of love that torched the whole room and left destruction in its wake. Only ashes and a fake number scribbled in lipstick on the mirror afterward. Vikram expected love to last for a lifetime, unfurling like a flower that wouldn't fade with time or season. When they pursued the same woman, it always ended in disaster-- that is to say, in Ashok's favor.

But Sahana seemed different. If she were the sort of woman who loved as he thought she might, she and Vikram were soulmates to be sure. It couldn't be a coincidence, the way he felt about her only moments after seeing her. She was bewitching, a woman made of light who shone above him like the sun. He had to get to know her. He had to try. No matter the cost or possible embarrassment.

Vikram laced up his shoes before he realized what his hands were doing. He grabbed the notebook he always kept on his person and locked the door on his way out. He took the stairs two at a time, skipping a little as he jogged his way back out into the street to catch the closest cab. He checked his watch at least five times between his apartment door and the closing doors of the cab he'd hailed. It normally took about forty minutes to get back to the M.R. Enterprises office, a little longer in rush hour traffic. But if he were lucky, he'd be there to catch her on her way out the door. From there, what would he do? Offer her a drink? Offer to walk her home? Ask her what she meant by complimenting the book he was reading?

He might read her a poem.

But when he got there his worst fears were realized. He pushed open the glass doors of the sales department to see Ashok catch Sahana's wrist in his hand. They stood there for a moment, their gazes locked, still and pretty as a portrait, with his finger on her pulse. Everything froze around them, the whole room breathless and icy cold. Vikram felt it in his throat as though the wind had been knocked from his body. There was no air in his lungs for the duration of the time that Ashok held her hand in his. Had it been that easy? Were they fated for failure all along?

The book in his bag seemed foolish, incapable of shielding his heart from the hurt he felt erupting within him. He tried his best to quell the feeling. She was her own woman, beautiful and independent. He didn't know her. He didn't need to know her, no matter what the aching in his heart said. This could be a mistake that God prevented him from making. Another one of Ashok's games that stung like a bee sting, but in the long run, it saved him from a horrible relationship. He was moving too fast, thinking too much, doing what he always did because of his foolish pursuit of real love, a concept that might not even exist--

Then her hand slipped out of Ashok's grasp, and she shook her head. It was a clear withdrawal. A rejection. Something Vikram had never seen Ashok face before. Every bit of her body language shut him down, and Vikram felt his lungs fill up with air once more. She wouldn't fall for Ashok's false charms and shallow charisma. She was beautiful with such fire in her, it would burn away all his untruths and impurities. It heartened Vikram as much as it scared him. A woman like that was the sort of woman who only fate would allow to love him. He could do nothing to woo her if fate wasn't on his side.

She was staring down at Ashok but when her eyes fell on Vikram, her gaze softened. A smile flickered on her lips, sparking something within him that he couldn't quite name. Slowly, with caution, he approached her. Her smile widened as he stood in front of her. "Back for one more round with the staircase?" She asked, and he grinned at her greeting.

He raised his hands up in mock surrender. "I took the elevator this time," he said, wagging a finger at the stairs, "burn me once, shame on you. Burn me twice."

"He's wiser than you let on, Ashok," Sahana teased, and Vikram felt his heart drop a little as Ashok took it in stride.

"Book smarts, but not an ounce of imagination to him," Ashok complained. "That's why I keep him managing the office. Nothing slips through his fingers unless it is a metaphor or a bright idea."

Sahana hummed as though she did not believe him. "Ashok wants to talk more about the sales department's strategy for the new quarter over drinks at a cyber hub. I told him I'd only go if I had a chaperone. What do you think?"

"I think--" Vikram started, but he was interrupted.

"Vikram's a good country boy," Ashok said, "Hates to disappoint his mother so he barely touches a drop, and when he does? Let's just say he's a lightweight." Sahana laughed. Vikram felt himself give a mirthless chuckle to fill the silence. "Vikram, since you're back at the office, I need an update of the current projects spreadsheet," Ashok added. "It shouldn't take long if you start now. We may still be there when you're finished."

Vikram swallowed a sigh. This was what he got for slacking off. He should have known it would turn around to bite him. Torn between the job he needed and the girl he wanted; his mind was at war. The choice his heart wanted to make was not the choice he knew his brain would choose. "You guys go on without me," he said and powered up his laptop. Sahana lingered at the door for a minute, as though there were something she wanted to say. Vikram looked up expectantly at her, but couldn't know what was on her mind. Because the next moment, Ashok ushered her into the late afternoon sunlight.

Four

The sun made its way towards setting as the day progressed. It bathed the almost empty office in a thick, orange light. Vikram didn't even notice its beauty today. He just stared at his screen as he filled in the fields in the Excel spreadsheet and deleted duplicate records. It was rhythmic, thoughtless work. Perfect for a daydreamer and deep thinker, and Vikram would have indulged in it any other day. But not today, especially not when Vikram had something dark on his mind.

He could have easily worked from the bar where Sahana and Ashok were having a drink. But he'd been excluded as soon as he'd been invited. In spite of his concerns, he'd dug himself the hole he was in. The honorable way to escape it would be to do the work that would make Sahana's life easier – he knew Ashok asked him to update the current projects status to share with her. Even if it also benefited Ashok in the process.

The problem with this line of work, Vikram thought, was that it allowed him too much introspection. Perhaps if he were a farmer in the field, working with his hands and plunging them deep into the earth. Maybe then he'd spend less time living in his head, theorizing and daydreaming until he lost track of what life looked like.

After finishing the update, Vikram printed out a series of reports and stacked them in a manilla envelope to place on Ashok's desk for the next morning.

Then, checking his phone to make sure of the time, he printed out another set of copies to place on Sahana's desk. The copier groaned with the effort of having to do anything at all. Each page took its time coming out, hot to the touch when he ran his hands over them to stack each set into a report.

It was a waste of precious time that, in the short term, he could use to pursue her. But in the long run, it was a preventative measure. Give Sahana all the information she needed, and she wouldn't need to ask the sales department for a report she could read from her desk. One less trip to Ashok's sales floor was one less time she had to interact with him. Some time to sit apart from him and consider the sort of person he was. And if Vikram was lucky, it would give her some time to think of him.

Did she like him? It seemed to Vikram that she did. She had been the one to extend the invitation to drinks towards him, even if Ashok had excluded him. Vikram didn't think she'd invited him along because Ashok had been too pushy. She seemed disappointed when Vikram had to turn down the chance to spend time with her.

She was curious about him, he could tell from her gaze, the way she tilted her chin and raised an eyebrow when he spoke. He thought about her expression when he'd agreed to finish the reports for Ashok. Disappointment had been evident, easy to read. He wondered how hard Ashok had pushed, and if he'd ignored the rejection spelled out on her lovely face.

He hoped if he finished this last task, he'd be able to see her, but it was hard to say. He couldn't imagine her spending any more time around Ashok than necessary, so their "date" wouldn't last long. If he walked in the bar the moment she was leaving, he wondered if she would smile at him. Would she stay back to spend some time with him?

But she must be on her way back home by now, to an apartment he couldn't help but imagine walking through in his mind. One lined with books that stood in stacks where her shelves overflowed. A poster on the wall from her university days, now framed, but still crumpled from the many moves she'd had to make over the years. Boxes left to unpack in an apartment she was renting. Post-it notes by the phone with a reminder to call the plumber and her father. He imagined himself like a detective, collecting evidence of her that could fuel his poetry for the rest of his life. Her jewelry on the sink, the imprint of her fingers smudged on the mirror.

How she fascinated him. He wondered what it would be like to get to know her, to feel the anticipation of a new relationship, and let it blossom into full form. He let his eyes close for a moment in imagining. When he opened them, the sun had dipped into a warning red sunset shade. It struck him with a sense of anxiety when he realized how late it had gotten.

To her office then. He knew the marketing floor well. He often ended up having to visit there at least once or twice a day to drop off something Ashok was too busy to do himself. His friend Nalini, the office manager for the marketing department, worked on this floor. He'd often stop by her desk on her lunch break and message her on WhatsApp throughout the day. He'd taken over her duties when she was on maternity leave, and the two of them had been close friends ever since. So, he could find his way around the marketing office blindfolded.

Dropping off the reports, paper-clipped for her perusal. Looking around her office to see if she was settled in yet. Then making a quick sweep past the bar on the off chance that she and Ashok were still there. Watching Ashok make a fool of himself and lose any favor she might feel towards him forever. Heading home to read or to write another poem. The sunset was fraught with promise, and the thought of seeing her tomorrow sparkled in his mind's eye. In spite of what felt like a series of losses, Vikram felt as though he were coming out on top. He almost skipped as he made his way to the marketing department.

He swiped his key at the door and entered the now deserted marketing floor. There, push-pin boards full of concepts and rough sketches. Copy and creative posters decorated the wall like a teenager's bedroom-- if teenagers had ever been passionate about pharmaceutical sales. It was messy and creative. It was exactly the sort of department he would have loved to work in, if he'd ever been allowed to choose for himself what department he could manage.

The marketing people tended to be more cluttered than sales people. They were more creative than confident, and it showed in the details of their office lives. It was easy to understand them from the remains they left behind on their desks. Nalini, for example, had photos of her husband and children. She also had an incense burner, aromatherapy lotion, and a tin of half-eaten biscuits indicating she was stressed. A roster of internal phone numbers by the phone, scratched and scribbled upon in blue pen, and a flyer for a babysitting service that she'd scribbled her husband's name on, with an arrow pointing to the number he should call.

Marketing included graphic designers and copywriters. They were artists and thinkers and a great deal of people who did community theatre on the weekends. Vikram wondered how Sahana fit into this.

The answer was one he gleaned from a single glance at her office. She was a poetry person. She had framed quotes on her wall where other people might have pictures of their family or friends. She read not only Indian poets but French and British as well. Her shelves held volumes from Japan and South Africa and Mexico. She was worldly and seemed to feel a particular penchant for romantic poetry around the turn of the last century. How fascinating, to think of her love for modernists. Lost men falling in love on the brink of independence and world war.

He'd suspected as much of her, but the confirmation of it warmed his heart in a way he hadn't expected. A kindred spirit in this soulless office. It wasn't enough to make him look forward to Mondays, but it did make the prospect of Tuesday an alluring one.

He wasn't sure what made him do it. Maybe because Ashok thought he was defeating Vikram by taking Sahana out for drinks. In reality, he'd gifted Vikram with an insight into what sort of incredible woman Sahana was. This emboldened Vikram to make a move he might never have made otherwise. All the talk of fate and romance had gone to Vikram's head, and he liked the buzzing feeling, full of light and joy. He wasn't thinking straight when, after placing the reports on Sahana's desk, he fished his notebook out of his bag and tore out a poem from within its depths.

> *woman inspires universe*
> *to leap to life and imitate her*
> *hides the seasons in her skirt*
> *dances the pattern of raindrops*
> *into the soil as dark as her eyes*
> *a riot of red-lip flowers bloom*
> *under the spring in her step*
> *sun sets and rises*
> *to the fall of her chest*
> *her heart beats*
> *a rhythm of endless days*
> *I want to live in her time*
> *for the rest of mine*

Vikram's heart fluttered. He felt shy as he exposed the soft curves of his own handwriting to her eventual analysis. Would she know it was him? Would she find his words worthless, or use them as some sort of exercise, tearing it apart and editing into something more pleasing to her? He wasn't certain. She might find the last couplet of the poem too personal, too revealing. It might be that he was coming on too strong. Or maybe the poem was too obscure, and she wouldn't find it strong enough.

Maybe he should tuck the poem back into his notebook and walk away. Maybe he should crumple up the poem and throw it away, never to be seen again. But it was a good poem, and one of many that Sahana had inspired in the few hours he'd known her. It felt like knowing someone you'd never met well with one conversation. It felt a little like falling in love.

Thinking about what might go wrong would only bring him anxiety and frustration. Thinking about the things that could go right, however... Vikram wasn't sure how that made him feel. Excited and as anxious as any other thought did. Nothing had changed in his life for so long. Then, like a hurricane, like a dawn, when he'd expected only darkness, here was Sahana. Beautiful and thrilling, unleashing an unexpected flood of words and passion. He'd never believed in love at first sight and wasn't sure he believed in it now. But there was something about her that he couldn't let go. He wanted to know her, but he wanted her to know him too. He wanted her interest. He enjoyed her gaze. He wondered if her thoughts were of him like his were of her. If she felt as shocked and confused and excited for the future as he was.

Maybe she didn't. Maybe she hadn't noticed. Maybe she never would. But if he left that poem on her desk, at least it would ask a question. At least it would be a start.

Without another thought, he placed it on top of the reports and walked away.

Clocking out always took too long, which he thought seemed ironic. It would save the company money to streamline the process. He walked as fast as he could without breaking into a run through the streets congested with people. Ashok had chosen a bar further away from their office. He might have done so to make the day more difficult on Vikram.

It was no surprise to him that when he finally got there, neither Ashok nor Sahana were there. Still, he felt some lingering disappointment at Sahana's absence. Some foolish part of him hoped that she might have lingered there to see him. But no doubt, Ashok would have gone where she followed, unless she left him and headed home alone. Vikram hoped, at least, that she was alone. Sitting on a couch, talking on the phone while a pot of rice simmered on the stove. Reading a book, or writing in her own notebook. He was attracted to the thought of her as a reader. Her as a writer? The very premise was too tantalizing for him to think about. What if she returned his poem with one of her own on the next page?

Even though she wasn't there, the promise of tomorrow lingered in the air. The thought made his gut churn even as he looked forward to it. He'd made a bold and risky move in leaving her the poem, one that felt out of character to him. He wasn't a risk-taker and he never had been. But if this was a taste of what knowing Sahana could do to him, he felt like he might grow to like the person he'd become while seeking her approval.

Five

An email popped up in his notifications when Vikram signed into work the next morning. He felt a pleasant churning in his gut, excitement and anticipation mixed with a bit of dread. He thought for a moment that one might be from Sahana. He hoped she was acknowledging the poem he'd written, or asking him to drinks without Ashok thrown into the mix.

But unfortunately, and much to his disappointment, it was from Ashok. While it mentioned Sahana's name to brag about how well he'd gotten to know her yesterday evening. He walked her home, but he didn't get to know her too well, he insisted in his email. Ashok's reasoning was because he was respecting her as a lady and as his equal. But given he wasn't allowed in at the door or given a parting kiss, Vikram relaxed a bit. Even though Ashok saw it as a victory, Vikram did not think of it as anything more than a soft defeat. Sahana was being polite. She wasn't in love.

*

A couple of weeks passed in a haze – but not for Vikram. For Vikram, they dragged mercilessly pining over a woman he could only love from a distance. Sahana settled in well, and Vikram tried his best to support her in terms of any sales department related work.

He had hoped for some gesture in response to his poetry he had left for her, but nothing came. Maybe she didn't like it, he thought.

He was still in a dilemma about her feelings for him. He longed to talk to her, discuss random things with her. Sometimes even dreamt of sharing his feelings, but he didn't get any opportunity. The only interactions he shared with her were casual waves or random smiles. However, little did he know, things were about to change. Because, almost two months after Sahana's arrival, he received the weirdest email ever. It was from the CEO of the company, Mr. Azim Patil. It was addressed to Vikram and Nalini in marketing, titled: *retreat*. Unlike Ashok's constant bragging, this was abnormal and a little chilling to Vikram as he hovered over it, dreading to open and read the email.

"Retreat." Mr. Patil had a frightening way of popping up with sage advice on topics he shouldn't know anything about. He was a little kooky but had an eerie way of predicting the future that put him ahead of his competitors. Was he making a suggestion about Vikram's current situation? Anticipation turned to anxiety as he opened it.

Mr. Patil was a master of duality. He was a doting uncle-type to his loyal employees. He particularly loved the Chandigarh office, the first branch of the company he'd started nearly forty years ago. But he was a tiger when up against a fierce competitor. There was a strange aura to the old man that both inspired and intimidated all who worked for him. Ashok's goal was to be like Mr. Patil, but he couldn't quite manage to strike the balance between goofy and severe. It inspired fondness from those in positions to do Mr. Patil favors, and fear from those who could do him damage. It was why he was one of India's 50 richest men.

Mr. Patil tended to heap affection on the heads of his various departments. Vikram thought he hoped it might inspire some sort of trickle-down fondness from department heads towards the rest of the staff. As a result, Mr. Patil and Ashok had some kind of a father-son bond that Vikram tried hard not to envy. Mr. Patil ignored assistants and support staff until it was time to give a generous holiday bonus. Then, he'd treat Vikram kindly enough in a financial manner that he wouldn't mind being ignored for the rest of the year.

Vikram's faith in Mr. Patil was a little shaken while reading the email addressed to him. He wondered if the CEO had fallen ill with a high fever, or been hit over the head with a blunt object. Because the idea in this email couldn't bring anything but trouble to his beloved company.

The suggestion: Vikram and Nalini, his counterpart in marketing, would work together to organize a retreat at a nearby campsite. Its purpose would be to foster a strong bond between the marketing and sales departments. This was in light of Sahana's recent transfer from the New Delhi office.

Vikram would rather have been sent out in the wilderness alone to be eaten by wild beasts. Tigers never forced you to do icebreakers before they ate you.

If they were quarreling school children who needed to build camaraderie, it might have worked. But they were all adults working towards a common goal. Ashok might let his amorous pursuits ruin his life on the weekend, but he rarely let it get in the way of his work. He was a good boss, just a terrible friend.

But if Ashok were kept in cramped quarters with Sahana, they'd either fall in love or fall apart. Vikram was hoping for the second. And he hoped he might be there to see the fall out when it happened. The chance to pick up the pieces might allow him to build something good with Sahana.

Still, he worried the relationship between Sahana and Ashok might wreck. Then the bond between marketing and sales would sever in a way they couldn't repair. And if that bond grew cold, the whole company would suffer. M.R. Enterprises wasn't a giant, soul-sucking conglomerate. They didn't exploit or hurt people in the name of profit. They were charitable to a fault, especially when it came to education. They devoted millions to development in poverty-stricken places that might otherwise see no hope.

Vikram didn't organize spreadsheets and set up calendars because he needed a paycheck. He did it because, if he was honest with himself, he loved the work that his company did and loved his part in it. In its own sad way, M.R. Enterprises had so far been the love of his life. And he didn't want to ruin any aspect of that.

No one wanted to be forced into heinous icebreakers and team-building activities, but for Vikram, that wasn't what scared him most. He was nervous about seeing Sahana outside of the sterile office environment. The thought of her in the stairwell with her pinned back hair and glossy polished demeanor thrilled him. It was enough to inspire poems on his page and send butterflies fluttering in his stomach. He couldn't keep his mind off the thought of seeing her in the moonlight. What would she look like silhouetted by the stars listening to the soft whisper of wind in the trees? What if she turned towards him, a smile on her face, as she studied the beauty of nature all around them? He worried what he might do, what he might say to embarrass himself in a situation like that. If seeing her for brief moments during office time was enough to inspire him to write poems, what would it be like to see her outside of work?

Still, what better opportunity would he be afforded to get to know her? This was one that Vikram knew Ashok wouldn't be able to sabotage. He was too afraid to intervene in issues where Mr. Patil was involved, for fear of looking bad to the boss. Vikram was invited along on this trip. In fact, he was a key member of the team, required to make things work during what might be a tense retreat. There would be no leaving him behind or keeping him busy until the day he received an invitation to Ashok and Sahana's wedding. This would be the perfect time to get to know her and see if they really were a good match.

Of course, Sahana and Ashok might also find out they were the perfect match. But Vikram didn't want to think about that.

Instead, Vikram buried himself in editing and preparing a schedule of possible events for Mr. Patil's approval. He sent several WhatsApp messages to Nalini throughout the day. The marketing department knew how to throw a party. Word was already spreading through the office in whispers and pings from the internal messaging system. The office was abuzz at the prospect of a paid long weekend, but some grumbled about having to work during the time they might otherwise have off. There were plans of who would bring drinks and who would bring the hangover kits. Some asked questions about who might end up bunking with whom. The office rumor mill was so loud that Vikram heard the door open when Sahana walked in. When he saw her, the air rushed out of his lungs.

He couldn't help but admire her and wonder how lovely she was, all dark reds and straight lines. There was a sense of competency in the way she dressed, the way she walked that had to be purposeful. She was beautiful by design, but underlying all that was a beauty that was all her own. Something she'd been born with, some quality she might not even know she possessed. A curl had slipped from her pinned-back hair. She seemed a little unconfident, standing there on the floor of an office that was not hers to command. Then her eyes met his, and all the nerves slipped from her face. A smile replaced it. She looked happy to see him. Vikram wondered if he wore the same goofy smile.

Could she feel the way he did? Could she feel the same passion that he felt? A passion for which he had filled in endless pages with poetry?

Slowly she approached him, and excitement bubbled in his stomach. It has been days since they interacted. He hoped for something romantic, something poetic, but the words that fell from her lips weren't poetry. They weren't inspiring or loving or something he wanted to hear. Instead, she asked, "I need to meet with Ashok. Is he available?"

His heart soared to new heights every time he was around her. But he crashed further each time he realized she was still standing on solid ground. "He is," Vikram said, voice softer than he'd intended. "He's free right now, if you'd like to go in."

He expected her to immediately go to Ashok. Instead, she lingered for a moment, her fingers tapping the edge of her binder. He realized that a familiar sheet of notebook paper was sticking out of it. It was the poetry he had given her all those days ago. She had kept it. She seemed a bit perplexed by it, her fingers hovering over its edge like she might pluck it out at any moment. He didn't want to meet her eyes. The notebook from which that paper had come was sitting there on the desk for all to see.

But she didn't say anything about it, wrapped up in her own thoughts. The poem stayed sealed in her binder. "I wonder," she said finally, "what your opinion is on all this nonsense about fresh air and the great outdoors. It's been flying through my inbox all day, and I can't decide what I think."

A surprised laugh caught in Vikram's throat. "Well," he said finally, "do you like the outdoors?"

"Yes," she said at once, "I do. I love the time in nature and the connection it provides. It clears my thoughts and makes me think about life the way it was meant to be lived. I am always the better for it. It's the ice breakers and forced bonding that concerns me."

"Me too," Vikram agreed, feeling the ice between them cracking with the warmth of her voice. "I always worry it creates more tension than it's meant to do."

"I agree!" Sahana laughed, "And conflict is the last thing that we need right now. I like a natural connection, easing through the silence by pursuing a common goal. It's shown me a lot more benefit than playing trust-falls and telling interesting facts about yourself."

"Right!" Vikram snapped. He thought about the many conferences he'd attended where they wasted valuable time trying to get to know people to whom they'd never speak again. "My name is Vikram and I'm a poet. But that fact doesn't affect the life of anyone in this company, and will never be useful outside of small talk at the office holiday party. Your turn."

He realized what he'd said only moments after he said it. No amount of biting his tongue would allow him to hold back the secret that had tumbled from his mouth. Sahana was a smart woman. He could see the gears turning in her head as she came to the realization he wasn't sure he wanted her to have. Many poets in history were anonymous-- most of the greatest, in fact, were. He envied them in that moment, those known for nothing more than the words on their page. He could feel Sahana sizing up what she'd read, comparing it to who she saw before her. He wasn't sure she liked the comparison.

He didn't get the chance to know, nor did she get the chance to ask. At that moment, Ashok popped out of his office with a slick smile plastered on his face. "Sahana," he purred, "what a pleasure to see you. Please, come in for a moment. I've something I'd like to discuss with you."

The look in her eyes didn't immediately change to disgust. In fact, Vikram thought, there was no mistaking the flicker of interest in her eyes as she took in Ashok in his bespoke suit. His haircut cost more than Vikram's shaggy cut would cost him all year. She liked him, much more than Vikram realized. She seemed charmed by him in a way that Vikram hoped she wouldn't let herself be. Her nervous mood hadn't been over wanting to stay away from him, it was clear. Instead, she seemed downright interested in coming closer to him. He couldn't help but wonder if anything went down between the two over the past couple of weeks. But if something did, Vikram was sure Ashok would have rubbed it Vikram's face numerous times.

Vikram refused to let his heartbreak over something that destiny had intended to fail. He'd shown her his heart, and she hadn't found it wanting. Instead, she found something more appealing about Ashok's sleek charm. That was her prerogative. He couldn't change her mind.

Or perhaps it was all an act, he thought. He took a sip from the hot mug of tea at his desk and settled in his chair, watching his coworkers milling about. Perhaps she didn't like either of them. Maybe she thought of herself as above them, with her big-city ways. It was hard to read her, knowing her so little and wanting to know her better. Vikram lived too much in his head and too far away from her actual thoughts to know the truth. He couldn't profess true love to her, but he couldn't sit back and let her get away as well. He couldn't assume that he knew her thoughts well enough to decide whether or not to pursue her further.

It was only a moment later when Sahana exited Ashok's office all the doubts about her feelings towards Ashok evaporated from Vikram's mind. She was clearly annoyed. Her nose twitched with irritation as Ashok followed her out. His honey-smooth voice was layered on thick, no doubt trying and heal some offense he'd caused. When she thought no one was looking, Sahana rolled her eyes. Vikram laughed at that, burying his face in a wad of papers in front of his desk to hide his amusement. As the door slammed behind Sahana, Ashok leaned on a sorted stack of papers on Vikram's desk. The motion sent them toppling onto the floor.

"She loves me, she loves me not," he sighed before leaving his mess for Vikram to clean up. Vikram didn't mind the insult, unable to hold his laughter. He must have seemed half-mad, crawling around on the floor and snickering to himself. But if Ashok was fool enough to misinterpret Sahana's steely politeness as falling in love, Vikram had very little to worry about.

Six

The lunchtime rush was full of people on their way to a variety of tasks, very few of which actually involved eating anything at all. Running to the post office, to put more change in the meter, to hair appointments and dentist appointments, to take sick kids home from school and to run various errands. It amazed Vikram. He worked as an assistant only to Ashok and to himself. So many high-level executives were also assistants to their families and friends. What it amounted to was that the cafeteria was often a bustling mess for the first fifteen minutes of a break, then deserted for the last half of it.

Vikram rarely saw the cafeteria as anything other than a place to collect his thoughts and a plate of food. He wasn't leisurely about his lunches like Ashok, who had Vikram order from restaurants that served four courses and cocktails. Sometimes he wouldn't return for hours. Vikram never begrudged his disappearance, because it meant that he could do some work uninterrupted. Vikram ate at his desk, messaging with Nalini about what their bosses had been up to and how her family was doing.

But today, something was off. Nalini was slow to respond and responded in one-word answers when she answered at all. He wondered if Sahana was running her ragged. They were trying to get everything in place before their retreat. "Am I bothering you?" he asked.

"No," she responded. "Tired," a moment later. "Bored. Nothing happening around here."

"Same," he said, sending a yawning emoji to her. Ashok was gone for the afternoon and all his calls were forwarding to Vikram's desk. One young woman had called in a huff, demanding that Ashok return a t-shirt she'd left at his house. She hung up even angrier than she'd started. Besides her, no one remarkable had phoned. It was a Thursday, boring and slow.

"Why don't you take a lunch break?" Nalini asked him. "A real one. Sit down there in the cafeteria for a moment and actually taste your food for once?"

"Because then I'll realize how bad the cafeteria food tastes," he shot back, snickering.

"I'm serious. Consider it as a mindfulness exercise," she said. "Who knows what you might find. Change the scenery, and it might shake some inspiration free for your poetry."

"Why are you being so insistent about this, LOL?" he messaged back.

"No reason." she typed it too fast.

"Uh-huh." he typed back, sending an emoji making a skeptical face back at her.

"Until you try, you'll never know!" she said.

"LOL fine," he shot back. "BRB"

"You'd better not be right back!" she replied.

With a book tucked under his arm and change for the soda machine tucked in his trouser pocket, he whistled his way down to the cafeteria. Nalini's bizarre insistence that he comes down to the cafeteria to eat made no sense. That was, until he found himself behind Sahana in the lunch line, and realized how clever his friend had been.

"Oh!" Sahana said. "Vikram. How nice to see you! I was hoping someone I knew would come along. My cook took an off today, and I confess, I couldn't find time to know what a good restaurant looks like around here. I figured that starting at the cafeteria would be as good of a baseline as any."

Vikram laughed. "I suppose, start at the bottom and work your way up." He was glad that she joined in. The light-hearted sparkling quality of her laughter was enough to warm his heart.

"But in all truth," she said, "I always wanted to come down here and spend some time getting to know this place from the inside out. Only a true understanding of the office's culture and values will allow me to market us best. Even the taste of the cafeteria food lets me know a little bit more about my coworkers and how they live."

"They live poorly on days when they have to come down here to eat," Vikram said, "but it's a reality that could be worse. I ate worse in school."

"All *dal makhani* and *roti*," Sahana laughed. Vikram blinked in surprise. "Ashok told me about it when we were getting drinks on my first day here. He had a lot to say about you."

49

"Oh, no!" Vikram said, with a little less humor in his tone than he'd hoped to project, "Don't listen to a word he says."

"Alright, alright," Sahana said with a smirk. "I'll forget everything he said about how you were such a good friend. I'll forget that you're such a competent assistant that you attend to his needs before he even asks you. I'll forget that you were a shy, studious undergrad who worked hard and still made time to be there for his friends. Even when they did something stupid like, oh, what was it he said he'd done? With a bottle of flavored vodka and some co-ed from the United States who'd come to India for a semester abroad in microeconomics?"

"I'm not sure he should be talking about that. It was probably illegal," Vikram groused, but he couldn't help but feel warmed that Ashok had spoken so highly of him. And he couldn't believe the fact that Sahana had remembered so many details about him, even after so many weeks. He felt elated at the thought.

"I have no doubt that a lot of the things that man has done are illegal, but I do like that he owns up to all of it. He's very straightforward."

"I think of him as quite manipulative," Vikram countered. He didn't mean to sound so harsh. After all, Ashok had told her all good things about him. But it was very hard not to feel defensive when Ashok had made his intentions so clear to Vikram. He feared Sahana might not be aware of them.

"I see both in him," she added thoughtfully as she selected a drink and brought her tray up to pay at the register. "I understand. It's part of being a salesman. I knew lots of men like him back home. There are friends that you can love, but cannot trust."

"How are you finding life in the north?" Vikram asked, desperate to change the subject. He grabbed silverware from the metal canisters that held them and placed them on his tray.

"It's..." she trailed off, fishing out her wallet and paying for her meal. It seemed as though she were collecting her thoughts. "I know I'll grow to like it more," she said finally, "but it's difficult, sometimes, to make new friends as an adult. But I'm resilient. I'll adjust."

"I admire your work ethic very much," Vikram confessed in a rush. "It's something I've been meaning to say. From what I've heard from the people in the marketing department, you are the best."

"You've been talking to Nalini, then," Sahana said as they sat down across from each other at the flecked lunch tables. Vikram nodded. "I try to be the best. There's nothing else to do but work towards that goal, with family and friends far away. Even when I was still at home, I put work first. My parents were always happy that I chose books over boys, but they didn't give me much of a choice. Their expectations were so high. But now, even when I'm finally free to live a life for myself, I prefer living like that. I choose to work and strive to be the best. Also, I like it here. It's full of potential. I could do anything. Be anyone."

The force of her passion was like the summer sun beating down on his face. He loved the excitement with which she spoke, the interest she showed in becoming her own person. He had never seen her as perfect. But to view her like this, as a woman creating herself, was far better than any "perfect" woman could be.

"You have quite a bit of wisdom to you, beyond marketing knowledge," he remarked. She seemed a bit surprised to hear him speak. He was, in his own way, surprised, too. He found he could listen to her forever and not say a word.

"Thanks," she said, a slight blush to her pretty face, "I suppose I do a lot of reading. Some of the wisdom there sticks. I spent so much time in school reading. I learned a lot about understanding character and motivation observing book characters. It's useful in marketing, yes, but I find it useful in all interpersonal relationships. Not only the ones where you're trying to sell something."

"Huh," Vikram remarked. It was going to be another lunch hour of not tasting his food. He was too distracted by Sahana to enjoy or not enjoy the food on his plate. Her conversation was far more satiating than anything a person could cook. "I don't mean to offend, but do you consider that dehumanizing in some way, thinking of people as characters?"

Sahana took in his comment, listening with intent. Her reply was well measured. "On the contrary, I find it a very useful way to humanize someone. There are people who I might otherwise ignore, with little thought as to who they are or why they do what they do. It might seem cold and calculating to people who aren't avid readers. But some of my favorite people are the characters in storybooks. I've known them longer than many of my friends, and they've stayed constant and true. I find it a compliment to see someone as if they were in a storybook. I find stories are full of grace and forgiveness in a way that real life isn't always."

Vikram nodded, taking another bite of food he didn't care about. Sahana's voice, laying out such interesting thoughts, was the sweetest sound to his ears. "I understand what you mean," he said. "Though I'd never thought of it that way before. That may be why, in my childhood, I spent so much time buried in fiction books. Even in a world where there were monsters and dragons, I found that fictional world kinder than the world in front of my eyes."

"It's why fantasy is such a wonderful escape for so many people," Sahana agreed. "But instead of leaving it in the books, I like to bring it back to earth. Getting to know people, I think about them like characters. For example, take Nalini, someone we both know. I'd say that she's a woman who became a mother young but learned the sort of patience and inner-calm that skill requires. She's devoted to her family and finds tending to their needs to be one of her greatest joys. Though she is often bored at work, she does not despise her job. It gives her the ability to provide for her family as they grow up."

Vikram blinked. "She's said as much to me before, though not so eloquently, of course."

Sahana continued, "But even if she hadn't said it out loud, it's something you can observe. You see it in the way that she decorates her desk with pictures of her husband and children. She makes sure that people at the office have what they need. She is willing to do a lot to rearrange a schedule if someone mentions the words 'family emergency.'"

"I can see that," he said. He was scraping the leftover bits of food on his tray from side to side now. He didn't want to have to get up to put it away just yet, ending such a delightful conversation.

"Now, take you, for example," Sahana continued, speaking quickly so that he couldn't stop her as she outlined for him exactly who he was. "The only thing decorating your desk is books and piles of paper, always showing that you're in the middle of work. You're efficient, sure, but beyond efficiency, you put in long, hard hours whenever you find them in your day. At work. After work. You'd have to, to keep up with the demands of a boss like Ashok. Your relationship with him is complicated, but your loyalty above all keeps it functioning and in place. However, as hard as you work during the day, at night, you have to escape just as hard from the boredom of your office hours. You don't hate your job, but you're growing to resent it. Because there's no change in your life. You're too busy at work to take time to talk to others, and you go home to a lonely life. Am I right?"

Vikram could only nod, amazed. If it weren't true, he might be offended at being laid bare like that. But from Sahana, such careful analysis, as harsh as it was at some points, felt like a tender kiss.

"I wonder," he asked her, "how a character like me might work alongside a character like you?"

The moment hung between them, perfect in the air. It wasn't something he could take back, and he wasn't sure he would have if given the opportunity. He wasn't sure what it was about Sahana that made him so bold. But her smile, like the dawn, peeked across her lips.

"I wonder," she said.

Before he got the chance to find out though, his phone rang. Then hers did, as well.

"Vik, old buddy!" Ashok's obnoxious drawl on the line made Vikram want to hang up. "Just got a call from Mr. Patil. He needs to meet with you, Sahana, her assistant, and me this afternoon. He says it's urgent."

Vikram looked up at Sahana, still on the phone, shrugging helplessly as she mouthed, *I know, I'll see you later.* The perfect moment hanging in the air had shattered, leaving nothing but regret in its wake. Frustrated, Vikram trudged back up the stairs.

Mr. Patil was standing outside the doorway to the sales department when he got there, checking something on his smartphone. He did not notice Vikram for a moment. Vikram wondered if Mr. Patil recognized him at all, or thought of him as another faceless worker.

"Ah, Vikram," Mr. Patil said, smiling as he turned his face away from his screen. "I'm glad to see you received my message. I trust this day is treating you well? That smile on your face would certainly say so."

Unconsciously Vikram traced the shape of his lips with his fingers, he indeed was smiling. He hadn't even been aware of his smile, but it felt as though it were splitting his face open. He was slightly embarrassed to feel so unprofessional in front of his boss. Grinning like a goon, acting like a fool, falling down the stairs, and tripping over his own two feet every time Sahana was around. "I've had a great day, Mr. Patil."

"Wonderful," Mr. Patil continued, looking behind Vikram's shoulder. Vikram didn't need to turn his head to see what was wonderful. He could smell a puff of Sahana's perfume and feel the warmth of her presence. "And I see that Ms. Bhat is here. How are you enjoying our cafeteria facilities, Ms. Bhat?"

"They're quite to my taste," Sahana demurred. Vikram knew she hadn't tasted any more of her lunch than he had. He tried to keep his smile pinned back so that Sahana could not see it. She reached out to shake Mr. Patil's hand, but her eyes were on Vikram. Vikram felt his cheeks heating up. He wanted to say something to her, to tell a light joke or to confess all of his thoughts to her. But he couldn't think of a thing to say in front of his boss. Mr. Patil's eyebrow raised anyways, but he said nothing. Vikram was grateful. It gave him the ability to collect his own thoughts, and smooth the edges of his wild smile into something more professional, less intense. He had to remember where he was and what he was doing.

"I'm glad to hear that." Mr. Patil said. "And glad to see that you've already made connections in the sales office that will make this upcoming weekend so much easier. Vikram here is one of our most dedicated employees. Ashok wouldn't be half the salesman he is if it weren't for Vikram's solid support."

"Mr. Patil!" Vikram exclaimed, surprised. He'd never heard such high praise from Ashok, much less the leader of their entire company. He was content to work without praise, and embarrassed when he received any. But to have been given two strong compliments in as many days, both in front of Sahana, felt like some sort of sign. It was as though the whole world was trying to convince her to like him. He could only hope that she was willing to be convinced.

Mr. Patil only smiled. "Nalini Chander will be joining us once she finishes up her conference call with the New Delhi office. Ashok is already in his office. He says the pot of coffee with our names on it is already growing cold. Time is wasting and this weekend is fast approaching. Shall we join him?"

Seven

Mr. Patil took Vikram's favorite chair in Ashok's office, but Vikram didn't dare complain. He stood, shifting from foot to foot, as Sahana took her seat, and Ashok took his customary spot behind his desk. He felt a little awkward. He could feel Sahana's gaze on him, and he liked the sensation. He wanted to say something to her, no matter how difficult it was to form words around her. He wanted to retreat to his desk to daydream until he thought of the right thing to say to her, but he didn't dare close his eyes for more than a blink while Mr. Patil was speaking.

"I'm calling you all to this meeting because I wanted to go over our plans for this weekend," Mr. Patil said, templing his fingers as he spoke. A gesture that would have made Vikram look demented made Mr. Patil look distinguished. "I know that we all want this bonding trip to provide fruitful results, none of us more than I do. But that will involve hard work and dedication on all of your parts. I know that I can rely on you. You've been dedicated members of this company, of this community, for some time now."

"You can count on us, sir," Ashok said with a smile meant to inspire confidence. Mr. Patil gave him a gracious nod as he continued.

"I know it's Thursday, and we don't have much time before people leave on Saturday morning, expecting a retreat that will inspire them with confidence and boost the morale of these departments-- ah, Nalini, there you are."

Nalini shouldered open the door with a stack of stapled papers in her arms. "I'm sorry I'm late, sir, but my call went over and printing these took forever." She passed one out to each of them. She winked at Vikram as she walked by, then took a seat at the chair he'd left open for her.

"Now, as you can see, Nalini has provided you all with the initial copies of the itinerary that she and Vikram prepared. I've signed off on it and think it provides us many wonderful moments for bonding as a team. Starting Saturday afternoon, once your employees have checked in, we all will start off this retreat with a picnic, catered by the campsite facilities. It will be simply wonderful to enjoy nature and a nice meal after a packed train ride and shuttle up to the campsites. From there, we'll retire to the banquet hall and partake in some of the small group bonding and team building activities. There will be a hike in the evening, and then we'll all retire to our separate cabins. Sex segregated, of course, though I know that pains you, Ashok."

"I'll be nothing if not professional," Ashok retorted. Vikram couldn't help but roll his eyes. Before Sahana came in, Vikram might have believed Ashok. But since she'd arrived, his friend had been making a fool of himself at every turn. It was unprofessional and embarrassing at best. It would end with his firing at worst. Of course, Vikram had to be careful himself. Sahana was not a game. She was far too incredible, and her feelings were to be respected.

"I expect as much," Mr. Patil said, "After all, I'll need you fresh the next morning when you give a joint presentation with Sahana about the future of your departments and how you plan to move going forward. After that, we'll have another lunch in the banquet hall, spend the afternoon in small group lessons on our new database system, and the internal messaging system updates. Then, to shake the cobwebs off, I thought we'd have a dance in celebration of all the work we've done this weekend before we retire for one more night of restful sleep. Then, sendoff brunch in the morning and the day off on Monday to thank you for all your hard work."

"That's incredibly generous, Mr. Patil," said Sahana in a voice that gave Vikram the impression she thought it was anything but.

"To get all this done though, I need to ask a favor," he said. And here he looked to Vikram. "I'll need someone to go down to the campsite tonight in order to be there bright and early on Friday morning. You'll be able to spend the day with your boots on the ground, as they say, making certain that everything's in order. I know you've worked so hard already, but I need both Sahana and Ashok here in order to make certain both their departments are running smoothly enough that they can be ready for a long weekend. And Nalini, you've been so generous with your time already, but you are a family woman, and it would be best, I think, if you could spend some time with your children before leaving them for the weekend."

"Thank you, Mr. Patil," Nalini said. "I'm excited for this retreat, but I will miss my family."

Vikram felt a pang of envy in his gut. He pushed it down and tried to listen.

"And thank you, Vikram, for agreeing to do this on such short notice," Mr. Patil said, although Vikram had not agreed to anything at all. He did not want to leave a day early, especially considering it was so late in the day already. He'd have to order a ticket at the station and leave immediately to do so if he wanted to catch one in time. He was yet to pack his bag, and now he would have to find a bigger one to fit in extra day's worth of clothes and books. And that would leave him no time to speak to Sahana.

"You're welcome, sir," Vikram said. "I'll just need to pack my things."

"Absolutely," Mr. Patil said. But he made no motion to adjourn the meeting. "Nalini, you may also go," he said, "but I have more business with the heads of your departments. I wish you luck, Vikram, and will see you on Saturday."

With a dismissive nod, he banished Vikram from the room. Vikram could not so much as say goodbye to Sahana, whose back was to him. He could see the tension in her shoulders. He wondered if she wanted to run to him as much as he wanted to run to her. To get a proper send-off. To kiss her goodbye.

As he packed his stuff, getting ready to leave from the office, Vikram paused for an extra moment. He could feel the clock counting down until his train would leave the station, but he had to do something to say goodbye to Sahana. Anything that he could do to say goodbye in the way that she deserved. The office door was still closed and she probably wouldn't be out in time for him to do anything more than kiss her as he dashed out the door, and he wanted to take his time with their first kiss. Instead, he emailed her his number, along with a poem.

Fear died in my heart
the moment your light
illuminated my path.

All the questions buzzing
like wasps in my head
cut their stinging quips
and quieted.

All my worries
Evaporated
like rain on pavement.

Darkness couldn't last
against your smile
the sunlight,

Sahana.

Vikram checked his phone, swearing at the time. He didn't have time to think about his actions. He ran out the door.

The train ride down to the campsite was a lonely one because his heart ached for Sahana. Her response to his email had contained her own number but no other information revealing sentiment or even a sliver of her heart. He knew it would be unprofessional to do so, and she was nothing if not professional. Still, his heart felt torn open with every mile the train moved away from her.

Despite all the bustling noises of people on the train, he could hear his own heartbeat, alone in his chest. Vikram felt cold in comparison to the people around him, all of whom were making their own way to destinations he'd never visit and homes he'd never see. They all had families and love stories he'd never know. He'd never be able to write anything close to the warmth of an evening with family after a long day of work. He imagined what it would be like to belong where they lived. He closed his eyes and imagined what it would feel like to open the door, travel-weary and tired, to a warm pot of food on the stove. With his eyes closed he could almost feel what it would be like, greeted with a kiss and the sound of children's laughter. It seemed so impossible, there in that train car, that he might ever feel that.

His own family had been quiet, but the love they had for each other permeated the walls of their small home and enveloped him in a sense of security. He missed them. He should go home to them more often. But his mother's silent sadness every time he came home alone was enough to keep him away. Until he could prove to her that there was more to his life than just work, and add his own light to his parents dimming days, it felt cruel to bring his shadowy self by, begging them to replicate a love he should be building for himself at this age.

His finger hovered over his phone, Sahana's contact open in his lap. She was probably off work by now. The sun dimmed in the sky, hovering towards the sunset that would plunge the whole of India into the same balmy night. They'd left each other with so many things unsaid. He could just call her. He already missed her voice.

But he couldn't seem to get his voice to work. He cleared his throat, imagining the sound of the dial tone when he lifted the phone to his ear. Imagining her voice on the other end. "Hello?"

There was something blocking his throat, keeping his words from coming out. It was his heartbeat, too loud for anyone listening to hear anything he could say.

So, he opened a text message instead. He was unsure of what to type, but he typed it anyways. His heart knew the words his throat could not speak.

We need to talk. He deleted the text as soon as he typed it. *I miss you. I wish you were here next to me. I imagine you curled up, warm against my side, with a book in your lap, ignoring the world as cities swim past us both. You could be my whole city, my world inside a person. When I am next to you, I feel as though I am home.*

He deleted it again.

The train is crowded, he wrote, *all these people, and none of them is you.*

He sent it before he could say anything more.

The train rolled to a stop, and he realized this was where he was meant to deboard. Struggling with his luggage down the narrow stairs, he stood on the platform for a moment before he realized no one was coming to collect him. The crowd thinned as darkness encroached like a cloud of smoke dissipating in the wind. His phone rang, but it was just the driver the company had arranged to pick him up, telling him that he'd arrived. It wasn't a very long drive to the campsite, but it felt that way. He pressed his head against the glass of the window and drifted into restless dreams while he rolled even further from Sahana, imagining her dozing next to him as they traveled on. The world around him was pitch black night, illuminated in patches by the glow of streetlights and stars. He couldn't see the beautiful scenery in the darkness. The only thing beautiful was the woman he dreamed of-- and she lived behind his eyelids for the time being.

When he got there, the man at the front desk welcomed him and offered to take his luggage. "The campsite manager will be here in the morning. You can go over your organization's plans for the weekend then," he said.

He showed Vikram to a cabin with four twin beds. He'd be sharing it with Ashok as well as two other men from the marketing department. The cabin was austerely decorated, but the sheets were fresh and the facilities were clean.

Spreading out across the bed, Vikram kicked off his shoes and pulled the thin sheet around him. He was nearly too tired to undo the buttons of his shirt or shuck his trousers. His limbs felt heavy and his heart felt hollow. He ached with want and desire, fueled only by the dreary dreams he'd had of Sahana's hand in his during the car ride to the campsite. He had to force his eyes open when his phone buzzed, sitting on the nightstand without his charger plugged in. He rectified that situation while he opened the text. It was from Sahana.

My home is empty, her text read. *All these rooms and you are in none of them. I feel you farther away each moment. Like a string between us tautening with every mile you cross. I'm drawn to you. I can't help it.*

Then come to me. He responded.

I'll be there soon, she told him. *But for now, try to get some sleep.*

Her assurance was all he needed to drift into a restful sleep. She met him in his dreams.

In his dreams, she wore a dress made of the moon that wrapped around her in a swirling mass of silky light and smooth shadow. She grinned up at him with starlight glittering in her eyelashes, cool and beautiful as her smile faded, and her lips pressed against his in a perfect kiss. He could feel the slide of moonlight like soapy water through his fingers as he reached out to grab her. She dissolved into the rain. When he woke to the rattling of the wind against the window, Vikram did not feel as though he were sleeping alone.

Eight

Vikram awoke on Saturday morning before the sun was all the way in the sky. He padded out, barefoot, from the cabin where he'd spent another lonely night that hadn't been so lonely after all. Sahana had become his constant companion through the phone, and though he'd left her as just a coworker, she would be arriving this morning as a friend, if not a little something more. It was a wonder to see the pale rays of morning light peeking out behind heavy clouds as Vikram stood outside, breathing in the misty air and listening to distant bird song. It would be a beautiful warm day, if it did not storm.

At that moment, if everything was going according to plan, his coworkers were boarding a train. In rowdy clumps, they'd sit and laugh about things that they'd fumed about just the day before, allowing it to roll off their backs. Someone might pass around a flask, which most would refuse with a laugh, and some would sip from surreptitiously. They weren't being observed. Mr. Patil had taken a private car the whole way there so as to let them blow off steam before uniting with them for the weekend.

Sahana, for her part, had packed three books and planned to read for the duration of the journey. Vikram knew this because she'd asked his opinion on which ones she ought to pack. In the end, they decided that she ought to pack them all. If nothing else, it would give her more excuses to ignore Ashok, who'd told her that he'd claimed her as a seat buddy since Vikram had already arrived. In truth, Ashok had confided to her that he was nervous about their joint presentation and wanted to go over some of its finer details with her. Sahana wasn't certain if it were a front or not, and Vikram couldn't say for sure, either. He didn't want to disappoint Sahana with his cynicism about his old friend's intentions, nor did he want to leave her defenseless against Ashok's plans. So, he merely said that it was up to her to use her best judgement. In return, she'd retorted that she liked to gather all the reliable information she could before forming an opinion. And that she valued Vikram's knowledge more than many others. Vikram hadn't been sure what to say to that. It was hard to put into words the warm feeling that blushed across his chest whenever she gave him a compliment.

Many women had given him compliments about his appearance. He didn't dress the vain, peacock way that Ashok did. He didn't spend hours on grooming his hair into an artful coif. But he was attractive enough, with a nice face and a good-looking body. Old girlfriends had told him so in many different ways. His cheekbones, in particular, were a quality to admire. Women liked his eyes, his hair, the sound of his voice, the way he laughed. Still, it was one thing to be complimented for the way you looked and an entirely different thing to be complimented for your mind. One was being looked at. The other was truly being seen.

Distance had given Sahana and Vikram the ability to see each other. They had communicated only through texts so far. Each was too nervous to call the other. They were afraid it might break whatever spell was cast between then. They'd talked long into the night about literature and work, about the way they'd been raised and the things they'd grown to value once they made it out on their own. Loyalty and respect were virtues to them both, and they held them in high regard. "Love couldn't blossom without them!" Sahana said and Vikram agreed. They also valued the ability to honor a commitment, whether or not it was something you wanted to do. Their days moved in similar ways even though they worked on very different tasks. The key was this: rigorous discipline, augmented with a heavy regiment of daydreaming to get them through each day.

"Sometimes, I think that's why I'm so lonely," Sahana said, "I live so much of my day inside my head, making up stories. It can feel so real that sometimes I forget that I'm only talking to myself."

"It's hard for me, too," Vikram replied, staring at his glowing screen in the dark, "remembering that the person I'm dreaming of isn't actually right in front of me and doesn't know my thoughts or feelings."

"I know them now," was Sahana's reply. Vikram grinned until he fell asleep. When he woke up, his face ached, and his heart raced with the knowledge that soon he'd see her again.

The shuttles rolled in just as Vikram was swilling the last sip of his second cup of coffee, dressed and ready to greet them. When he'd welcomed Mr. Patil just a half-hour earlier, he was still blinking sleep from his eyes. Mr. Patil had been immaculately dressed, his suit unrumpled in spite of the early hour and long car ride. Vikram knew he needed to amp up his game. He'd dashed into the kitchen to throw cold water onto his face and ask the cooks how the progress for the picnic was coming along. The smell had been the only answer Vikram needed. They were in for a feast.

"My only concern is the weather," the head chef said to Vikram as he peered out the window. "That storm cloud is moving fast and might pass us by entirely. Or it might open up the heavens and send rain gushing forth, ruining all of your plans."

"I'll see what Mr. Patil thinks," Vikram left after assuring the chef.

But his boss was all ready to welcome an onslaught of rain as a refreshing reminder that they were close to nature. "Smell that breeze! There's no forgetting that we are close to nature and far away from our desks." He confided to Vikram, "besides, I believe the cloud will pass us over. I'm rarely wrong about these sorts of things."

Vikram was not so sure that he agreed, but he quickly forgot his worries when Sahana stepped off the shuttle. Her hair was loose and ran in rivulets down her back, beautiful as a crow's wing and nearly blue in the sunlight. Her dress was far more casual and befitting the natural surroundings. They were not at work now. And the lightness to her shoulders, the confident and cheerful way she carried herself as though she were a younger girl and not just a high-powered executive, inspired Vikram. He wanted to run to her, to grab her hand and go darting off into the woods. To chase her down as though they were children. To play and romp through the weekend, enjoying nature, just the two of them.

Then Ashok's hand clamped around his shoulder as he said, "Hey, buddy," and Vikram nearly choked on his irritation.

"Did you have a nice train ride?" he asked his friend, hoping that Ashok would say he'd had food poisoning or had to sit next to a shrieking baby the whole time.

"Sahana and I sat together and worked on our joint presentation," Ashok said. "I think you'll find that after all the time we've spent together in your absence, the two of us are really in sync."

"Are you?" Vikram bit back. He could barely hide his smirk. He felt his life was beginning to syncopate with Sahana's with each passing day. When they spoke, they fell into an easy rhythm, the sort you couldn't force by sitting next to someone on the train or subjecting them to your presence every minute you could. Ashok's approach to romance worked for finding a one-night stand, hunting someone down like prey. But for love, it just made a woman feel cornered.

Sahana's eyes caught his. He gave her a wave, barely moving his fingers. Her face lit up in a smile warm enough to blow all the looming storm clouds away. She began to approach him, moving in an easy, relaxed way that invited him into her orbit. It felt for a moment as if the whole crowd parted, and she was the only person there.

Then Mr. Patil tapped on his microphone and began to speak. "If everyone could find a seat, please."

Vikram settled onto the nearest picnic bench as the kitchen staff brought out aluminum pans full of Tandoori chicken, tandoori kebab, paneer, and three varieties of salad. The rich smell of spices made everyone groan with hunger. Another table was heavy with bottles of wine and scotch to act as a social lubricant and as a reward for all their hard work. A mutter of approval went through the crowd as the aroma wafted across the picnic shelter.

Mr. Patil called them all to settle down. "I have just a few announcements before we can begin. I know you've had a long train ride, so I'll keep things brief. First off, I'd like to thank everyone for coming, and for our hard-working staff, Nalini and Vikram, who were instrumental in making sure this weekend could happen. Vikram, in particular, deserves a round of applause. He left home early to ensure that everything was ready for your arrival. And isn't it lovely out here?"

There was a round of weak applause which was drowned out by worried murmurs as Vikram's coworkers cast glances towards the blackening sky. It was beautiful out there, away from the stained concrete and dirty class of the city. Even the looming clouds couldn't dampen the joy that came from fresh air in their lungs, lightening their spirits and the weight of their work that showed heavy on their shoulders. But it certainly could dampen the spirit of an outdoor picnic.

"We'll talk more once we get inside and begin our bonding activities for the day. But let's make this a weekend to remember! Enjoy!"

There was a general sense of disharmony trying to line up for the food. It was clear that everyone was tired, hungry, and a little disheveled from their time on the train. "Excuse me," Vikram murmured as he bumped into someone.

"Not at all," Sahana replied, brushing her hand across his shoulder. She took her place in line behind Vikram as they heaped their plates full of hot food. "Pleasure bumping into you."

"The pleasure is all mine," Vikram said with a smile. "Do you like tandoori kebab?" he asked as he spooned some onto his plate.

"My mother made the best in the world," Sahana informed, "but I'm sure the version that they serve here will be inspiring."

"Inspiration is supposed to be the whole point of this weekend," Vikram shrugged. Sahana let out a laugh. "I'm sure it will be inspiring. With whom are you sitting?"

"I don't know how I'll be able to get away from Ashok for much longer," Vikram muttered.

"Me neither. We ought to stick together," Sahana offered, wrapping her arm around his. And with the smell of her perfume in his nose and the feeling of her body pressed against his, the way he'd wanted for so long, who was Vikram to deny her that?

He didn't get much of a chance to respond though, because at that moment, the first fat drop of rain fell from the sky.

"Rain!" someone shouted, and the next moment the shelter was abuzz. Everyone trying to fit under its tin roof as the sky opened up and rain gushed forth from the heavens, soaking everything around them. Thunder roared distantly and Vikram swore under his breath, trying to catch a stack of napkins that flew forward when a gust of wind. Everyone was caught up in the chaos, grumbling as they tried to put together a picnic that had been doomed from the start.

The only person not unhappy was Sahana. While everyone was trying to seek shelter where they could find it, in the midst of the rushing around and all the pouring rain, Sahana had done the opposite. Instead, she'd darted into the rain. She was now soaked to the skin, laughing with childlike wonder as the water caught in her eyelashes and dripped down her hair. The phrase "dance like no one is watching" had always seemed so cliché to Vikram until that moment. Seeing her there, it seemed like the only thing to do.

He wasn't the only one who thought so. Nalini, brave as ever, darted out after Sahana and splashed right into a puddle. It looked like so much fun, the girls whirling around as water flew off their dresses, splashing in the quickly forming puddles. Before long, half the team had joined them, Vikram included. He tried not to seem as though he were headed straight for Sahana, but the magnetism that drew him towards her was so strong. It was impossible to stay apart.

"Hi," he said as she kicked puddle water towards him. He could barely hear his own voice over the pouring rain, the laughter of his coworkers, and the pounding of his heart in his chest.

"Hi," she shouted back, whirling towards him. "Whoops!" he caught her just as she slipped. He could feel the warmth of her lower back against his palm. Her deep eyes looked up at him, hiding nothing. There was warmth and affection in her gaze, the sort that couldn't be denied. Before Vikram knew what he was doing, he was leaning in to kiss her.

It wasn't appropriate. It wasn't the time or place. But there in the middle of a rainstorm, he knew one thing for certain. He was in love with the woman in his arms. And the way she was looking at him, as if daring him to kiss her, he was pretty certain that she loved him back.

And it was for that reason that he pulled back, righting her before she whirled off again, continuing to laugh and splash as if nothing had happened. And even though his heart felt heavy with the profound weight of this new knowledge, Vikram couldn't help but smile. Soaked to the skin in the heavy onslaught of rain, he was happier and felt freer than he'd been in months. This was bonding, the sort that no ice breaker or weekend retreat could do for a team. Sahana had managed to salvage a potential disaster and turned it into a memory that would last a lifetime.

From the calculating look on Mr. Patil's face as he watched safely from inside the shelter, not risking getting his suit wet, Vikram could tell that he had noticed as much, too. Sahana wasn't just a brilliant marketer or an excellent worker, she was also an incredible leader. The sort of person a team could follow beyond their confidence in their own abilities, simply because of their faith in her.

Vikram wasn't just in love with her. He was proud of her, too. He could feel her on his skin, nearly taste their missed kiss on his lips. He'd have to talk to her, but there would be time to talk later. For now, he just stood in the rain, watching her dance, a poem blossoming in his mind.

Nine

The rain poured forth as though God was sitting on top of a paint ladder flipping buckets of water onto the people below. It fell in sheets, slapping hard against the ground in a roar. Thunder growled from high atop the black clouds. Lightning flashed across the sky in violet flames. It was like an earth bending storm. The soaked sales and marketing teams now sat safely inside the banquet hall. They ate what parts of their picnic had survived the dash back indoors. Now they gnawed at their kabobs and set aside their plastic tumblers of scotch, dissolving into idle conversation. The high of dancing in the rain had passed, and they were gloomy discussing the prospect of returning to work.

They seemed more settled, even though the artificial air conditioning made them tremble with cold in their wet clothes. They conversed with ease, sitting closer and smiling wider than they had on the cramped train. Where before they were coworkers, now they were new friends. The bonding was already well underway, stronger than any ice breaker could have made it.

That was the power of Sahana's leadership. Vikram admired the way she worked. Even now, she touched freely. She put a hand on Nalini's shoulder. She shook hands with a member of the sales department she had not yet met. Ashok made a joke and she slapped his wrist, her smile warm enough to evaporate the storm above them into a clear blue sky.

Vikram was in love.

With her power, her beauty, her wisdom, and her might. With the way she'd braided her dark hair, dripping with rain, and kicked off her shoes as she spoke. The conversations they'd had built up like dark clouds above his head. Finally, the cleansing rain of truth washed over him, and Vikram realized how he felt. He wanted to take her away from this, to sit with her alone and write and talk until everything was clear. But it wasn't necessary. He felt as though he could say as much to her with the touch of his hand in hers.

Mr. Patil clapped his hands and brought the whole room back to order. "Ladies and gentlemen, I'm grateful for your perseverance in spite of the storm. We're moving our activities inside for the day--"

"Which rather ruins the point of a nature retreat," Ashok joked, sliding into the empty seat behind Vikram. Vikram felt his shoulders stiffen a little but tried to relax.

"-- but we're going to get started with an activity I hope none of you have done in this office before," Mr. Patil said. His grin was very youthful for a man his age, "Speed dating."

"Otherwise known as your daily office behavior," Vikram shot back at Ashok. Outside of the office it was easy for him to give as good as he got to Ashok. It reminded him of their university years when they were on equal footing, life was less serious, and nothing had been ruined between them. It was amazing to realize how a few years have changed their relationship. He wondered how long it would take to heal them if they chose to start today. Could they, with Sahana between them? In the fresh air, even with the rain, Vikram felt more optimistic than he had ever felt trapped in the office. Even with the irritation he felt at Ashok's constant needling, it was easy to remember that they were friends when they were out in nature. That might have been Mr. Patil's goal.

"All the same department will line up on one side, and all the marketing on the other. You will each meet for two minutes, talk to each other, and find at least three common interests. At the end of your two-minute meeting, the sales department will move one seat to the left. Sahana on left end moving all the way to the spot that Nalini, on the right end, has vacated. So on and so forth until everyone has met everyone else and found a common bond."

Vikram groaned. This was exactly what he and Sahana had been dreading. It was clear that everyone else was thinking the exact same thing. The tension threaded through the room once more. No one liked an ice breaker. It made the room feel colder. Vikram could feel a shiver in his bones from the rain. He took his seat across from a man in marketing whose name he thought was Ram.

When Mr. Patil announced, "Go!" Vikram laid out a laundry list of things about himself. He was a poet in his spare time. He wouldn't watch a movie without a happy ending, which meant he'd spoil it looking online for the ending. He hated when people put ice in scotch and had ordered whiskey rocks to keep his own scotch from watering down.

Ram blinked. "I thought it was going to be more like a conversation, but women must like you a lot if you get down to the point so fast."

"I learned it off Ashok," Vikram joked, embarrassed, "no need to mess around if it's for fun anyway."

Ram developed a strange love for American country music and hadn't been able to shake it after university in the southern states. He had a green thumb and a garden on his patio, and he puts chai in his coca-cola. Then the timer went off, and Vikram moved on.

As he worked his way down the line, he remembered lunch with Sahana. He thought about the keen analysis she was able to develop by meeting other people. He wondered what she was making of this opportunity to learn and know people. The most of it, he imagined. He longed for her social graces and ability to make anything into a lesson, an opportunity for her betterment. Her open heart and ability to love people was something he wanted to imitate more than anything in his life.

So, he tried to listen, thinking of her all the while. He learned about people who had three children and people who never wanted any. He learned about vacation plans and parents and candy preferences. He met a woman who never wanted to touch an instrument again after a childhood spent trying to be a piano prodigy. He met a man who went to school for engineering to please his parents only to take a job as an artist anyways. There was so much to learn in behind every boring fact. Vikram found himself fascinated.

All the while he learned the pattern and rhythm of other people's lives in a way he'd never thought to pay attention. He learned to spot who was happy and satisfied with something in their lives. He learned to see who had holes in their hearts from childhoods scarce of love or loves long lost. It was strange how easy it was to love people when you looked at them this way. He thought of Sahana's own lonely childhood trying to please her parents. She stayed away from boyfriends and best friends in favor of working hard and becoming the best she could be. Was this how she'd learned to love instead? By looking at people from a distance and seeing the strange, beautiful whole of them? Was that how she'd learned to love Vikram?

Then she was right in front of him and he realized that no, the way she loved him was different and he could see it in her eyes. She'd learned to read people in prose, but they loved each other in poetry. How could they not? It was the language of love. Upon meeting each other, it was as though they'd been able to greet each other in a mother-tongue that hadn't crossed their lips in years. He realized what he hadn't the moment he fell down the stairs: he'd loved her on sight. His mind knew hers.

"Hi," he said, aware he sounded breathless. It was silly, the way love made him feel. As though every drop of rain that had ever fallen had nurtured a field of flowers, as though he'd woken up one day out of a dream to see them in full fragrant bloom. That was how he felt whenever he saw Sahana's face.

"Hi," she said. There was no need to state three facts about themselves. He could see everything about her in her eyes. She knew that and she felt it too.

"I'm Vikram," he said.

"I know," she said. She bit back a smile that threatened to crack her face open.

"Three facts about you," he said, and she blinked in surprise at the reversal of the tired old ice breaker. "You'd rather be barefoot than ever wear shoes and it's the worst thing for you about working in an office. You love poetry and stories by men living at the start of the modern world. It makes you feel like you've entered a whole new existence in which nothing is as you thought it would be. And three," he said, hoping he was right, "you're in love with me."

"Three facts about you," she countered. The grin she'd been hiding blossomed into full bloom on her face as she picked up the game he was playing. "Your favorite thing about being out here in nature is a cool, stormy breeze. I could tell the way you turned your face into it that it made you feel more alive than you ever looked in the city. Two: you read poetry because your soul craves beauty in this life. You're never quite able to believe the lie that sometimes the world is ugly. You find it in the pages when you can't even see it inside yourself. And three," she smiled wide enough to let the sun burst through the clouds, "you're in love with me."

"Well, that's three, then," he said. He could feel his pulse in his fingers. He wanted to place them on her skin.

"That's three," she said. Then the buzzer rang. "Vikram, you still need to keep moving. The ice breaker isn't over yet."

Vikram felt warm all over. "But I'll come back," he struggled to his feet and willed them to move. "We'll keep talking."

"I'm counting on it," she said.

The rest of the icebreaker passed in a blur. Vikram wanted to listen the way Sahana listened, but every time he thought of her name, his eyes darted back to her. He could tell that she was frazzled and distracted though she didn't look it. Her professional face was on. She would, every once in a while, tuck a little loose piece of hair behind her ear. For Vikram, it was a tell that gave her away. He imagined his hands being the ones to pull her hair back from her face. He wasn't certain how much longer he could keep going without his lips on hers.

"Vikram? Vikram?" the person in front of him said, "is there anything you'd like to reveal about yourself?"

"Ah, yes--" he said, trying to shake the sun out of his thoughts and bring himself back into the gloomy reality of the rainy room. *I'm in love.* He thought it. He couldn't say it out loud. He fished for something in his mind that didn't have to do with the warmth in his chest that was spreading across his cheeks. He tried to think something that wasn't Sahana's name. "When I'm flying, I like to order coffee and dip those biscuits in the coffee. I know it's a little gross. If I had to bring a book with me to read on a desert island, it would be a collection of poetry. One from many poets, in case I got bored with one's style and wanted to study the other. I can't stand ice in my scotch. I like to freeze whiskey rocks and put them in my tumbler instead so it doesn't dilute them." *I'm in love. I'm in love. I'm in love with Sahana Bhat.*

He knew it like he knew the color of his own eyes, like he knew the pattern of his heartbeat. Like his body knew to breathe without him having to think it. It was hard to remember inconsequential icebreaker facts when he had new truth living inside his body like one of his own organs.

He was a man in love. And the woman he was in love with hadn't even touched him yet. His body ached for it. But even without her touch, he could still feel her in his veins. It gave him a purpose that oriented him to the pattern of her breath, each movement her muscles made. The iron in his blood magnetized to her, the compass in his heart pointing towards her, his true north. He could feel the poem of her life ingrained into the grooves of his mind. He ached to be alone with a pen to write it all out, the things he felt inside of him.

He wanted to be home. With her at his side. This weekend couldn't end fast enough.

"Buddy," Ashok said at that moment, sliding his arm around Vikram's shoulders, "we've got to talk."

"Sure thing," Vikram agreed, pulling his mind back to the place he was and forgetting where it was he wanted to be. This was work. He could do this.

"It's about Sahana," Ashok said. Vikram's eyes narrowed. "Come with me out into the hall."

Vikram followed Ashok out, unsure of what his friend was going to say. He imagined that Ashok could tell that the game was his to give up.

"Sahana told me I could try it," Ashok said to Vikram.

"Try what?" he said, his mind unable to comprehend.

"I told her I was going to kiss her at the dance tomorrow, and she told me I could try."

"What does that mean?" Vikram asked, his mind swimming with confusion.

"It means you've lost, buddy," Ashok said. Vikram blinked. "And I've won."

"But..." Vikram thought about their conversation. He'd said she loved him and she hadn't denied it, telling him that he loved her. Was she correcting him? Had he misinterpreted everything about their interaction? Was it Ashok she loved?

"Sorry, pal," Ashok said. "Guess she wasn't the girl for you after all. We're resuming in five minutes. Go to the bathroom. Wash that look off your face." He clapped Vikram on the back at that and walked off.

Vikram felt the sunshine had been doused out of his heart and replaced with fiery hate for Ashok. He couldn't be sure that Ashok was right until he talked to Sahana. He'd been so certain of her love. He couldn't be wrong.

But Ashok had always been right their whole lives, a guiding force where Vikram's head had grazed the clouds. He held him to earth. To the earth that was not always pretty.

In the bathroom, he stared at his face in the mirror. It was not the one he could recognize, distorted with jealousy, uncertainty and pain. How could Ashok be the one that Sahana loved?

Ten

"You can't work with a community who you can't trust to hold you up," Mr. Patil spoke, unaware that he was ruining Vikram's life with every word. "So, we'll be practicing trust falls. Into the arms of your closest compatriots. Think of them as your brothers and sisters in arms as we move forward towards making this quarter our most productive sales quarter yet. I believe in you, but you must believe in each other. What more practical, instinctual way to show this trust than to practice trust falls?"

Vikram didn't trust anyone right now. Not Nalini, who he'd assumed had set him up to meet with Sahana that fateful day for a purpose. Definitely not Ashok who, with a couple of words and a well-timed smirk, could still cause Vikram to feel insecurity deeper than his faith. Not Sahana, who had seemed so true. He played over her actions in his mind until he couldn't remember what he'd actually seen and what he'd imagined after the fact.

His doubt would be his own undoing in the end. He couldn't help but be a pessimist in the face of love. How quickly had he built faith and felt it dissolve from under him? How quickly had he fallen into the old patterns of thinking he wasn't good enough?

Anger overcame him at that thought-- Ashok wasn't trying to ensure that Vikram ended up with a good woman. All he wanted was to make Vikram feel that he wasn't good enough for any woman, for any friend, for any job above assistantship. He liked Vikram as low as he'd been once his father had died and wanted to hold him in that low pattern. It made Ashok feel like the bigger man, the better man.

So no, Vikram didn't feel any trust when Ashok pretended to backflip off the table and into the waiting arms of the sales and marketing team. But he caught him nonetheless, as he always had. They'd been something akin to brothers once, and it was hard to give up that instinct to save, to protect. Hadn't that been what he'd doing, begging his friend to give up this endless game of women and noncommitment? But it was over now. They'd gone too far over the edge. Now, Vikram couldn't catch and salvage their friendship.

The question was if he could fall into Sahana and trust her to be there with him when he hit the ground. It would have been an easy enough game to play. But Ashok knew every place to hit Vikram: his jealousy, his uncertainty. He needed to believe that Sahana was special, not just to think it and feel it, but to know it with all of his heart. He wasn't sure if there was enough heart left to love her the way she deserved. To be a man without jealousy and fear. But she deserved that, didn't she? Someone who could love her above his own fear and self-interest!

He wasn't sure if he could be that person, but he definitely knew that Ashok could not be. Of the two of them, he was more suited to her needs.

Sahana now stood on the banquet table. Even in a room full of relative strangers whom she'd only known for a short amount of time, there were enough people in the crowd who would catch her. Above their duty to their friends, they were a group of people who liked her, who loved her. She was the sort of person who inspired faith and the protective instinct in all who met her. Vikram knew he needed to be the person who could truly save her as she fell. He stood front and center, his arms outstretched. With a smile and peaceful look on her face, she took the plunge with closed eyes.

It was as if she'd known he would be the one to wrap his arms around her. He could feel the heat of her shoulders as she rested her weight against him, opening her eyes to see him looking down at her. What a reversal of fate, to have fallen at her feet only to have her fall into his arms. There was something electric about it. Vikram felt they were the only two people alone in the room.

"We've got to stop meeting like this," she murmured, but he could tell by her smile that she didn't mind their meeting this way at all.

"We've got to stop ending up this way with other people around," he whispered back.

"Come on, you two, get up and let Vikram have a go," Ashok shouted in that loud, manly sort of way. It had been teasing in school but now it sounded juvenile, a little more sour than playful.

Still, the crowd cheered at seeing Vikram doing anything more physical than flipping the pages of a book. He was jostled up to the table where he climbed up gingerly. The electricity on his skin where his hands had come into contact with Sahana was starting to dissipate. The nerves he felt at Ashok's warning moved like fire through his skin. He didn't want to fall into these people. He didn't want to fall again.

"Come on, Vik, you're so good at falling," Nalini teased a little meanly. Vikram rolled his eyes and tried to act cheerful in spite of his own misgivings.

"Just for that, I'll try and crush you on my way down," he shot back.

"As if you're heavy enough for it to hurt," Ashok laughed. "Go on, buddy, light as a feather. Float on down to us."

"Vikram," Sahana encouraged in a quiet voice, and it was all he needed to tip his head back and fall.

A sea of strong arms caught him, much to his surprise. His coworkers. His friends. Sahana among them, Ashok among them, Nalini and all the rest. As much as he'd resisted understanding Mr. Patil's point, it had, in its own strange way, worked to comfort him.

He could see Sahana was pleased. As the group broke for supper before their night hike, he could see her smiling at the lot of them. She was pleased beyond her own expectations to see everybody getting along. Her grin was infectious. Vikram took two steps towards her, feeling the warmth of it. The next thing he knew he was flat on his face, tasting the wax on the newly buffed banquet hall floor.

Ashok's foot slid surreptitiously back into the crowd, where no one had noticed he had stuck it out. But Vikram knew, even through Ashok's syrupy false concern, as he picked himself up off the floor, who had done it. It wasn't an accident. His wrist stung a little.

"I'm going to run some water over it," he muttered, stumbling out of the room. In truth, only his pride was hurt, but it was harder to heal than a sore wrist. The only thing that might have hurt him more was a broken heart.

In the hallway, he paused for just a moment to breathe. His lungs felt empty, as though he couldn't get enough air in them. He turned around to see Sahana following him out of the banquet hall, concern on her face. He hated the look and wanted to do anything to wipe it away.

"You looked like you were in pain," she said, and he took her hand in his. He was suddenly unsure of what else to do. There was only one course of action that made sense. Her hand was warm, and he could feel her pulse fluttering like a bird in her wrist.

"I am in pain," he said, "every moment I spend waiting to kiss you."

She let out a quiet gasp. Then she took his hand in hers, "stop waiting, then," she whispered.

Vikram pressed his lips to hers.

It was everything that he had wanted for so long realized in one moment. He wouldn't have cared for the whole office, Mr. Patil included, to have seen him at that moment. It was the happiest moment of his life. Her mouth was warm and sweet against his, surprising him as he deepened the kiss. She responded with an arm around his neck as she stood on her tiptoes to reach him. She was so eager, her hot body pressing against his as the kiss turned hungry. It was all he could do to contain himself. But then her nails scraped the back of his neck, and he pushed her gently against the wall, leaning down with an arm at her hip to take her in as close as he could. Their breath mingled, hot and tasting dimly of scotch and wine. He hadn't felt drunk until he'd kissed her. Now he was intoxicated by the feeling of their skin touching.

Every point where their body connected was a point of immense heat. Desire pooled in Vikram's stomach as Sahana's mouth opened and licked into the kiss. It wasn't dirty, instead, it was full of more passion than anything else he'd ever done. In that moment, Vikram's mind was totally blind to language. All he knew was the touch of bodies, the feeling of Sahana's lips on his, her breasts pressing against his chest as she pulled him closer, muttering "more" into his ear.

He couldn't give her much more. Not here. Not without ruining her reputation. He knew that and she knew that. But it was hard to care when his teeth scraped against her lips, and he heard her moan. Knowing that she'd wanted him as badly as he wanted her was the highest he'd ever felt. He wanted to pull her into some closet, some place where they could be alone.

But where was the poetry in that? He felt poetry in the dance of electricity between them as Sahana shuttered. He felt himself breathing unsteadily, guiding her closer to him. He felt the tension in her body loosening, and her desire overwhelming him. He hadn't expected her to kiss like she was hungry, but then, hadn't they both denied themselves love for so long? Vikram with his insecurity and her with her focus. They met in a cataclysmic crash of need, and it was hard to stop.

"Not here," he whispered.

"Here," she insisted, her nails scraping down his back.

"Not now," he corrected, and she finally contained herself enough to pause in kissing him.

"Not now," she agreed. There was reluctance in her voice, but she put her hand against his chest. It was not to draw him closer but to push him far enough away that she could straighten where he'd mussed her clothing. There was a piece of her hair out of place. Vikram did what he'd been wanting to do since he met her. He tucked it gently behind her ear. Her eyes looked up at his through thick lashes, dewy as the morning and bright as the moon.

"But soon," she told him. "Tonight, while the others are on the hike, slip back to me. I've wanted this for so long."

Vikram nodded, "me too," he said, "since I first saw you."

"You were concussed when you first saw me," she rebuffed him with a soft laugh but pressed a kiss to his knuckles as she stepped away from him.

The excitement that thrilled through him was hard to contain. He was so close to pushing her up against the wall, but he had to be kind and careful. She'd unleashed something within him, some hungry lovesick animal that only wanted Sahana. He wanted to hold her down and let their bodies melt hard into each other until he couldn't tell her hair from the softness of the sheets in his bed. Until they were one body, tired and sated and secret and safe.

Vikram read poetry. He lived in novels. He knew the way that bodies could starve not just for food and for drink but for flesh, for the kiss of skin against skin, and he'd certainly felt it before. He was no blushing virgin. But with Sahana, that feeling was so intense that it was another feeling altogether. Stronger than addiction or want, something so strong that it could only be called love.

More than that, there was a strange sense of pride and smugness in him now that he knew Ashok had been wrong. He'd solved all of his questionings and agonizing by taking decisive action and beat Ashok to what he'd thought would be a deadly blow. He'd won Sahana's love, and he was certain of it, just as she was certain of his love. That couldn't be defeated by a note scribbled on a bar napkin or a well-placed smirk over Vikram's head. He was loved, finally. He was the sort of man who deserved to be loved.

"We have to go to supper," he told Sahana, and she released the hand she'd been holding for a beat too long.

"You're right," she nodded, "but after that…"

"After that," he agreed, and it was a promise.

Eleven

There is no doubt that my heart sings for you
My body like spring bloomed into a new life when it touched yours
You are the rain I have longed for one thousand years
My soul is all bird song and jasmine flower perfume
I taste a new song on my lips where you left your kiss.

I t was a short poem, but it was all Vikram allowed himself to write on the post-it note he slipped to Sahana at supper. No one had noticed his careful hand placing the note in hers, but the smile she'd sent him back had been so blindingly brilliant that it was a wonder no one had said anything by now.

The mountains at sunset were a beautiful place to stand. For all of Vikram's initial misgivings about the retreat, he couldn't be any happier to be where he was. Mr. Patil had been right that a little bit of an escape was all their company needed to feel refreshed and excited about the work they were doing.

He felt a little wild with the smell of the earth after rain, and with the memory of Sahana's kiss on his lips. He couldn't wait to get home so they could truly be alone, but for now, he'd settle for any spare time to spend with her.

The sunset seeped from the horizon and throughout the sky in pale pink streaks that blossomed into royal golds, deep oranges, and vibrant reds. The clouds had blown away after supper, leaving the drenched landscape muted in comparison to the clear, jewel-toned sky. Vibrant as a ruby, the red sky at night had everyone scrambling to get out into the clear mountain air after a day spent in the banquet hall. The misty breeze and the singing birds in the canopies were just mesmerizing. They wouldn't go far into the mountains-- not at night, not in any kind of remote wilderness. None of them had ever seen a tiger, but they didn't plan to start now. Still, a quick hike around the grounds would be good for their constitution after a long day. It would give them time to digest and time to play outdoors.

There was still a bit of childishness to adults after all this time. When faced with a mud puddle, the answer was to play in it. When faced with time in nature, the answer was to hop up and try to swing from the tree branches, scuff at the mud with your boots, and otherwise act a little silly. They chased each other like children and play wrestled. Someone had even brought a soccer ball to kick across the empty field in between the banquet hall and the cabins, and a couple of the men played an informal game, mostly passing the ball back and forth. Vikram joined them for a little bit and got bored. Ashok had asked about a frisbee but no one had one to pass, so he'd spotted in for Vikram in the soccer game after a moment. No words passed between them, even though Ashok looked like he wanted to say something as they crossed paths. The irritation he felt towards his boss must have been palpable.

Vikram was torn between gloominess and joy. He was leaving one friendship behind for a new and thrilling love, and while he could not be wrong in choosing Sahana, there was still something in his heart that told him that this decision would be difficult and not easily enforced. It was too easy to fall back into old patterns with Ashok, to rely on his friend to have his back and to guard him, even though with his new insight, he could see that it wasn't happening anymore. But he wasn't sure how to say that to Ashok, so he said nothing at all. He walked away.

He couldn't stand by Sahana either. It was like holding his hand just above a hot flame. Too close and he'd get burned. But still, he felt himself drawn to her, his gaze following her movements whenever he noticed himself looking. He wanted nothing more than to hold her in his arms. He could still taste her on his lips and smell the heady scent of her perfume every time he turned his head. It was as though she was still on him, her whole body and not just the heat of her gaze.

Nalini would notice that there was something off about him the moment she stood near him. It would only take her another two seconds to make him confess to what it was. She'd always been able to read him like a book, and even over supper she'd shot him quizzical glances, as if able to tell that something was different though she might not be able to put her finger on it. He wasn't sure if she'd be excited for him-- after all, hadn't she set him up with Sahana that one fateful lunch break? He didn't care to find out while things were so new.

Mr. Patil still frightened him more than he cared to admit, with his all-knowing gaze and smile that belonged on the face of a much younger man. Ashok was a shark. The others were strangers, coworkers, people with whom he shared nothing more than lunch breaks and coffee- certainly not something so new, so intimate. There was no one he could be near that wouldn't force him to give himself away. And he couldn't give himself away if he was going to see Sahana tonight. People at work couldn't know yet. With their clumsy hands and all of their talk, with Ashok's envy and Mr. Patil's cunning disapproval, it might crush the spring-new thing blossoming between them.

It would be a matter of minutes until he had her in his arms again, and then he could kiss her instead of driving himself crazy with the memories of the last time their lips had touched. As he set off on the hike, he comforted himself with that thought. He waited until the group was well on their way and entranced in conversation, paired off in twos and threes, to slip towards the back. Then he ducked downwards as they continued on, pretending to be fascinated by the pattern of a broad green leaf while the others turned around a corner on a path. When most of them were gone he ducked back the other way, jogging down the path so quickly he was nearly running. He barely noticed the beauty of nature all around him. He was so enraptured with the thought of Sahana's beauty. There was nothing he'd rather see on this mountain than the sight of her face smiling up at him before he took her lips in a warm, soft kiss.

And there she was, waiting for him when he caught a view of the campsite once more. He was faintly sweaty from the jog back to camp in the hot evening. She was beautiful, not a hair out of place. Sitting still by the banquet hall, winding a blade of grass around her finger like a ring, she sat there watching his approach. She had a book by her side and a smile on her face. She'd been able to get away from the evening hike by claiming a stomach ache and an interest in helping the staff clean up after supper. It had been a thin and flimsy excuse, but the fresh mountain air felt too good and kept the office from asking any strange questions that might have given them away. They'd escaped. They were free. There was nothing left to do but to figure out the rest of their lives together.

She stretched before standing, a long moment where he watched the lithe movement of her body. Her muscles seemed a little sore, as though she'd been waiting all of her life for him to get there instead of just fifteen minutes. He reached out a hand to lift her to her feet, and she immediately pressed her body against his, brushing her soft fingers against his cheek as she pulled him into a long, sweet kiss. They didn't need to speak when their bodies were so eager to do all the communicating. His skin practically sang with the brush of her mouth against his neck.

The earlier passion returned from their first kiss as their fingers tangled together, and he felt her gripping his hand hard, urging him to deepen the kiss. She needed him closer and closer still. And he needed her back. He was too happy to oblige, pulling her into his space. He could feel her against his thighs, his chest, grasping for every spare bit of skin she could get ahold of. One hand snuck under the hem of his shirt, her small hands resting on the bare skin, sending an electric thrill through him. Suddenly, surprising him with her strength, she pushed him hard and the kiss turned aggressive. His head hit the back of the brick wall, and he scrambled to pick her up as her legs wrapped around him. The pain sparked through him like heat. He didn't care. It felt good to feel her go wild.

This wasn't Vikram. He didn't let passion carry him away like this. He'd never had a kiss like this before in his life, one that demanded more from him than he knew he could offer. She took the lead wherever his body seemed to question what they were doing there and answered with a firm kiss that brought him back down to earth. Her body felt so good against his. Her skin was soft, and the curves of her body gave way to his firm hand, soft and sweet as she began to whimper. His knee slid between hers and she gasped. "Not-- here--" she panted in between kisses, all the while leaning in closer to him.

"My cabin," he whispered, setting her back on the ground. She didn't want to return to earth. She wanted to orbit through space with him. She seemed dizzy for a moment, as though she might fall over. Then he took her hand in his and she steadied, grinning up at him.

"No," she whispered, and he stared at her confusedly. "I have a private cabin, let's go there," she moaned as she leaned against him to kiss him more.

"Come on," he whispered, breaking off the kiss rather reluctantly, and they ran together. It felt so good to move through the night with her, before either of them had taken off a piece of clothing. Their bodies were already in sync, their steps falling together like the patter of rain on the dirt. They knew each other from skin to soul. All that was left to do was touch, letting their bodies melt together into one as they were longing to do.

They didn't make it into the cabin before she was on top of him again. Her cabin was in a secluded corner and had a small, private garden attached to it. The grass was moist and soft, but nothing was softer against the skin that was touching his soul. Her hand grazed his belt as if asking permission, and Vikram's breath caught in his throat. Maybe he ought to be asking her, to be a gentleman, to try and slow things down. A gentleman would lay her out on silk sheets and ravish her in the full light of a room, not take her under the moonlight. But the look in her eyes was white-hot and undeniable. She wanted him. He was along for the ride. And she wanted him there, now. He fell beneath her, and she overtook him, kissing like a starving woman.

There in the grass as the moon rose and poured forth its silvery light on the campsite, she straddled him, her fingers working over the buttons of his shirt until she could graze her hands over his bare skin. Her body was hot against his, and he wanted to feel her skin touching his. He reached for the hem of her shirt and helped it off her body. She grinned, thrilled, as his hand touched the hot flesh of her stomach. Her mouth was wet from their kissing and red from where his teeth had grazed her lip. She looked wild and beautiful, like a goddess who'd fallen from the moon to take him as her mortal lover. This was a mystical, magical moment. He felt as though he were under a spell as he reached to slide off her pants.

Their bodies rocked together like ships on the ocean tide, spurred into motion by the full roundness of the moon. He could taste her sweat as he brushed his lips across her collar bone. His hand tangled in her hair and the tug of it made her moan. He made an answering noise in the back of his throat, and she kissed it from his lips. They were far beyond words and negotiations now as he slid into her, feeling her back arch with pleasure as their bodies met. Each motion was primal and as natural as the grass beneath their bodies or the canopy of trees overhead. Vikram could feel Sahana coming ever closer as her hands tightened around his shoulders. Her gasps and whimpers drove him wild, and he lifted his hips to meet her with every thrust, feeling her fingers scrambling for purchase over his sweat-slick skin.

Everything felt hot and misty and unreal, like waking up from a dream into another dream. He felt a placid sense of peace about it even as white-hot heat ran through him. Sahana keened above him as he began to lose control of the rhythm of his thrusts, enveloped in her heat, in the desperate hitch of her breathing, in the scrape of her nails across his skin. She was everywhere, biting into his neck, panting into his ear, moaning as he used his hands to guide her on top of him.

This was exactly how it was supposed to feel. This was love, crazy, passionate and all-consuming. It was poetry in motion, the coupling of their bodies, each place their skin touched was a stanza about love and fate coming together in the sort of verse that the great poets could only dream of capturing with words. This was his greatest work, that first pairing of their bodies together. A collaboration of skin on skin, lips on wet lips, fingernails and kisses and dreams shared between two bodies touching. It was a masterpiece, the love they were making together.

After the tide receded, the moon seemed a little smaller. Its glow on Sahana's dark skin illuminated her, making her look otherworldly as she bit back a yawn, sated and loose-limbed. She rested her head against Vikram's chest. He breathed in the perfumed scent of her hair, intoxicated by its smell, by what they had just done. He didn't know who they were. They could have been any pair of lovers in history, desperate and sated and overjoyed. Her name left his lips without his even realizing it until she responded, pressing a kiss at the base of his neck where his collar bone was.

"Yes?" she asked, her eyes bright in the moonlight with joy and the knowledge of what they'd just done.

"I love you," he said, "that's all."

"That's enough," she said. He could feel her lips, smiling into his skin. "That's all I need."

Twelve

Vikram could keep his face straight, but his hands betrayed him. They were constantly drifting towards Sahana, doodling her as she spoke at their morning meeting, reaching to link his fingers with hers in the middle of the workshops they attended throughout the long day. He drummed them against the desk, daydreaming until the day ended and they were let off the hook once more to dance. He couldn't wait to hold her in his arms. With the wine and scotch flowing, in the dim lighting of the dance floor, perhaps no one else from work would notice if they danced together. Perhaps no one would care.

She was driving him crazy with every breath she took and every move she made. He craved her and could see on her face that she did too. He couldn't look at her beautiful face without remembering the way the moonlight highlighted her cheekbones and played across her hair. His hands wanted to rest at her waist, tangle into her beautiful silk locks, and trail against her hot skin. He wanted to touch her. Every moment spent anywhere other than in her arms was a wasted one. He was going crazy.

After they'd fallen together breathing hard in the grass last night, they'd used and *misused* the showers in the Sahana's cabin to wash the dirt from their hands and knees. It was a new experience, seeing her body in full light, the hot water caressing her skin as she shampooed her hair, staring up shyly at him through her wet eyelashes. Even in the strange artificial light cast in the showers, she was beautiful. It was intoxicating to see so much of her skin and to be allowed to touch it. Before he knew what he was doing, he had her pressed against the wall. She went easily onto her elbows, her laugh melting into a moan as he entered her again.

For all they'd talked and touched, they hadn't talked for sure about who they were to each other. That made Vikram nervous. It wasn't that relationships between coworkers were explicitly forbidden by the company, though they weren't encouraged either. But two people working in two different departments might as well be two people from two separate worlds. It could be a safe relationship, if none of their friends interfered to snip it before it could bloom. Knowing their friends and coworkers as well as he did, Vikram wanted to protect the delicate flame burning between them until it could consume them all with love.

As she and Ashok shared a speech that received a standing ovation from both departments, Vikram found himself completely taken with her. The room moved with her, their eyes following everywhere she went. Ashok, the peacock who'd never found himself lacking in attention, seemed to fumble for a minute, shocked at how the joint meeting was going. They only paid him attention when Sahana allowed him the room, and even then, they cast furtive glances back at her, warmed by the power of her passion and excitement whenever she spoke.

Vikram was among the adoring gazes, but it felt different. It was a privilege and a blessing to be the only person in the room who knew her best. She was attractive in the simplest way. He felt drawn to her magnetic energy as though he were made of metal. He'd never felt so alive as he had under her touch.

The lights dropped low in the dance hall as Vikram and Nalini put the finishing touches on the display board of sales records. Mr. Patil insisted that they would be an "inspiring decoration going back to work on Tuesday." It certainly wasn't a traditional dance theme, but alcohol was a motivator. Soon the room would be flooded with members of the sales and marketing teams, ready to shake the cobwebs out of their brains after an afternoon spent in lectures and various team-building seminars. Vikram had already poured himself a scotch in celebration of the best weekend of his life.

Then Nalini turned to him. "Vikram, I noticed you were missing on the hike last night."

"My stomach hurt and I turned back," he said automatically, sticking a ribbon on the display, "is that too much?"

"I noticed that Sahana was also absent from the hike. With the same stomach ache." Nalini said, shooting him a pointed look. "Did the two of you manage to fix it together?"

Vikram choked on his scotch.

"I'm not saying I know anything about anything I shouldn't," Nalini continued, "and you know me. I'm more observant than most of the goons around the office, so I should say that your secret is safe as long as you choose to keep it. But if you and Sahana are together..."

"It would be none of your business," he told her stiffly. It wasn't that he didn't want to trust Nalini with this information, but it was exactly what he'd worried about. Too many hands on a new love would break it in its fragile bloom.

"It wouldn't be my business," she agreed tersely, "but all I was going to say is that if you two are together, I'm happy for you. I know you, and I know Sahana. You've both needed each other since before you met. If you believe in fate, I'd say that you're fated to be together."

"And do you? Believe in fate?" he asked Nalini.

She smiled warmly, looking off into the distance. Her thoughts were no longer within the confines of this campsite. "My auntie forced my husband upon me. Wouldn't let me rest until I'd agreed to meet him for coffee. I realized when we met that he was the same boy I'd met in a computer science seminar in college, only now he was a grown man. He still had the same kind eyes. I couldn't let him get away, so we were married within weeks. I don't just believe in fate, Vikram. I live it every day. And I'm so happy to see your happiness."

"I am happy," Vikram admitted. It felt like a dangerous confession to make.

Nalini grinned. "Good. I know Sahana can seem a bit distant at times and I wonder what's going on in her head. But I think she'll be good for you, if you can both stick it out. Ashok will go on his way and the rest of the office will settle, and then it will be just the two of you and the rest of your lives. Don't mess it up until then, if you can manage it."

"I think I can manage that," Vikram said, "though I'm surprised you have such little faith in me."

"It's not that I have little faith in you. I've seen you work miracles in the boardroom. Ashok probably would have been fired right now if he didn't have you attending to his every need and making up for him whenever he messes up. But love is a completely different profession, and a skill set you'll need to learn."

"Do you think I'm hopeless then?" he asked her, unable to keep the self-deprecating frown off his face. "Am I incapable of making this love everything we want it to be?"

"I think you'll have to learn to work together with someone, rather than just to serve them. To listen instead of just obeying. That's the key to a true partnership." Nalini suggested.

"I suppose you'd know better than anyone," Vikram said. "Thank you for your advice."

"I felt like you could use someone to talk to," Nalini said. "It seems like it's been weighing on your mind."

"It's a happy weight," he said.

Nalini sized up the room, but Vikram was keenly aware of her eyes on him. She was sizing him up, too. He straightened his shoulders, hoping that he would not be found wanting of Sahana's affections.

"There we go," she said. "I think we're ready."

"As we'll ever be," he agreed.

Vikram signaled the DJ and the first track began to play, an upbeat dance number that was sure to pull everyone on to the dance floor. As though they'd been waiting by the door for their musical cue, his coworkers filed in. Some went straight for the dance floor, some went straight for the booze, others clumped up into groups for conversations that couldn't wait until Tuesday morning.

Sahana stood by the drinks, sipping a plastic cup full of red wine. Her smile was distant as she observed the people around her, pleased to be there. Only someone who knew her, as well as Vikram, could see that her heart was far away, searching for a place to stay. Then her eyes locked with his, and she was home.

"Would you like to dance?" he asked her, coming up to her.

"Why I'd love to," she said.

They couldn't dance together, so they danced side by side, excitement rushing through his body like a flood each time their skin brushed together. The swarm of bodies moving around them pressed them closer together with each song that played. Vikram loved music and felt his blood pumping to the rhythm of every song the DJ played. There was something incredible about fast songs, the way that they could feel the joy of the whole room pushing them closer together.

And then there were the slow songs. Those were the best and worst of all. The rhythm was perfect for a dance of bodies touching each other, and it was driving them wild. With every pulse of the beat, Vikram could feel his mind flashing back to their time in the shower, the way their bodies melted together under the hot spray of the water until the water turned cold. He remembered her breath intermingling with his as their lips brushed against each other. He could almost feel her kiss against his lips, even though their bodies were barely touching.

It was like they were the only ones in the room. Her eyes met his on the dancefloor, and the music muffled in his ears. He could hear the hitch of her breath melting into moans, the way she begged for more with his hands on her hips. He couldn't remember where he was, suddenly. It was all too much. He had to get off the dance floor or kiss her immediately.

"I'm going to grab a drink," Vikram was aware his voice sounded strange with the effort it took to seem as though his heart hadn't taken up residence in his throat "Do you want anything?"

"I can't have any more wine," she said, motioning to her empty cup, "I already feel drunk."

"I know what you mean," Vikram took her cup towards the trash can. His eyes didn't want to leave her face. His body wanted to press itself into her until they were one. He couldn't let that happen here. "I'll be right back," he promised, as he pulled himself from the crowd.

The air was still hot around him, but he was able to think once he'd removed himself from the touch of bodies against his skin. He gulped a plastic cup full of water, then another one. It did little to quench his thirst, but it gave his body something to do other than wanting Sahana so desperately that he could barely see. The DJ had picked up speed again, and the jubilation of the party was infectious. But Vikram had to remain in control. He couldn't let himself be pulled away into a dance that might lead himself to forget where he was and who he was with.

When he turned back to the dance floor, Sahana was not there.

His body knew it before his eyes had ascertained it. She was not where he had left him. He couldn't feel the heat of her gaze on him or sense that she was near, waiting for him, wanting him. Somehow, she'd moved, left, gone elsewhere without him. He could not track her down.

Around him the crowd pulsed and moved, all to one beat like working parts of a machine. Perfectly in sync. Mr. Patil would be pleased with what the retreat had done to increase unity between the once disjointed portions of his workforce. But Sahana, the heart beating in their body, was absent. Vikram didn't want to panic. It would be ridiculous to feel anything other than mild dismay at losing sight of Sahana. But something felt wrong. He couldn't decide if it was in his own mind, jettisoned by the nerves he felt at having someone to call his own, the newness of their love. Or if his instincts were trustworthy.

Maybe she'd just gone to the bathroom. He opened the doors of the dance hall and ducked out into the cool, air-conditioned hallway, gulping a breath of fresh air. The doors fell shut behind him, quieting the loud sound of voices and the pulse of the bass from the speakers. Vikram sighed happily, just to be able to hear himself think. The silence gave way to a muffled argument, somewhere down the hall.

It was hard to hear the specifics, but as Vikram approached, walked as slowly as he would to his execution, the first thing he recognized was that the voices belonged to a man and woman. Another two steps and he thought he knew who they belonged to. But at the third step, he was certain.

He couldn't make out what Ashok said to Sahana, but he could hear her reply, "you leave him out of this! Don't talk about him. Don't even say his name." It didn't sound as though she was playing, it sounded as though she was furious. He could imagine whose name Ashok had said.

They quieted, and Vikram rounded the corner just in time to see his worst nightmare playing out before his eyes. Ashok's lips were on Sahana. Just as he'd imagined, Ashok had taken and taken. Sahana's hair was in disarray as Ashok held her against the wall.

Vikram couldn't stand the sight. The sinking feeling in his stomach gave way to nausea. He wanted to feel furious, to punch Ashok in the face and tell Sahana how all his disappointments and fears had just been realized in that single instance, so soon after he'd finally allowed himself to trust, to feel love. He wanted to hurt her, to break her, to make her feel anything at all. But with Ashok's kiss on her lips, it was clear that she felt less than he thought she did. How had she managed to play him like this?

Vikram ducked out the doors into the night. The moon staring down at him was far more cruel than it had seemed last night.

Thirteen

The fire in your eyes branded me as yours
From the moment we met. When our hands touched
I learned that only you could pull the ache
From this burn, with your lips, with your kiss
Bringing sweet water to the scorch of summer.
I thirst for you like a desert remembers rain.
Only you, my love, will satisfy me.
I wait. I dream. I write.

Vikram read his own words in his notebook as he sat there in self-loathing. Oh, how he hated himself and everyone around him at the moment.

He started packing up his things in a haze, he wanted to disappear from the night and neither see nor show his face to anyone. But the first train out of this hellhole was not until morning – the train everyone else, including Sahana and Ashok, were to take.

'Was it this easy for her to betray him?' he wondered as he closed his suitcase and sat on his bed. It must be, why else she would have turned to Ashok the moment Vikram had walked out of the room? But he was so sure of her love. Why else would she touch him that way, kiss him that way? She'd been certain enough to press herself into his arms, to follow him to the grass by her cabin, to take him inside of herself and to whisper that she loved him.

He read the next poem in his notebook, another one for Sahana.

This train moves forward
Passing beauty I can't see
Cutting past towns full of faces
That matter not to me
My love is standing still
And this train moves fast away
I close my eyes to it and dream
Of being next to her today.

How stupid he felt now remembering the moment he had written it.

Hatred boiled in his veins now. If Sahana couldn't love him for who he was – even when he had opened himself to her like never before – then he wasn't capable of love.

Vikram picked up the pen and started scribbling in the notebook.

Lady liar,
Your mocking lips

Destroy me
With your smile

A snake lies sleeping
In a bouquet of roses
I inhaled your sweetness
And your venom with it.

You tear through me
Shred my fragile soul
Poison the well of hope
Once living within me

I die with the sting
of your last kiss
Hoping still
for a taste of your lips.

And there it was, four stanzas worth of a shattered heart, visible for all to read. It was what Sahana had done to him, quartered him, and cleaved him into bits with her unfaithfulness. Or maybe he'd done it to himself, with his stupid, foolish hope. In spite of her kindness towards Ashok and Ashok's own warnings.

Vikram had been avoiding seeing his reflection in the mirror. He didn't want to see himself at his lowest. He knew what he would see there would only be a reflection of a self-loathing and self-pitying man. But in turning his face away from it, he caught a glimpse of a man who shocked him. A man whose face was full of fury and sorrow, who looked wild and broken and just as hideous as he'd thought he might. A ghost that might frighten people as he walked back to the party.

Good, he thought as he let the door to the cabin slam shut behind him. *Let my face serve as a warning to them. Let them see what love can do.*

*

Vikram stalked back out towards the party. In the depth of the night, he could move through the omnipresent darkness without being detected, which suited him fine. The fewer people who could see the sorrow on his face, the fewer people who would pity him in the office on Tuesday morning. The black shadows suited his black mood.

In his hand, he held the shoebox of his broken dreams, stuffed with silly poetry that was useless to him now. He wanted to burn it all to the ground, but he wanted the bottle of scotch to salute their demise. The scotch would fuel the flames of his bonfire. There was no telling whether it would quench or feed the burning pain in his heart. The only thing to do was drink.

The party was now almost over, and people were working their way out of the dance hall and back to their rooms. Buddies with their arms slung over each other laughed as they stumbled back to their cabins. Girls waiting for their friends at the bathroom door with compulsively reapplied lipstick, even though the night was long over and they'd be removing it within minutes of returning to their rooms. The DJ was playing one of the final songs, and few people were on the dance floor. Vikram stood out in the cold, unable to feel anything but contempt for them.

No, it wasn't contempt. He couldn't manage that. It was an aching loneliness. Not just for Sahana, but for the friendship he'd once had with Ashok, now lost and far beyond repair. Because despite what Ashok had done in the past, Vikram was a loyal friend. He missed the camaraderie, kinship, years of common interests and time spent being there for each other. It hurt that Ashok had given that up over a woman, even one as incredible as Sahana. There was no healing that deeper wound. To have lost a best friend as well as a lover in one ill-fated kiss. That was the source of the pain.

Vikram was devoted to washing down that ache with a bottle of scotch when he heard the sound of a woman crying.

His heart ached as he recognized the source. He didn't want to go to her. He knew better than to approach her. But the animal magnetism he felt for her still had a hold on him, and he felt his legs moving without his consent towards her. Towards the only inevitable outcome. Towards Sahana.

She looked wrecked. Her hair was tangled and hung limply in a curtain around her face as she sobbed heavily into her knees. When she lifted her perfect face to look at him, he saw that her makeup had streaked her face in shadows, and her lipstick was smeared across her face. This wasn't a façade... this was sorrow, real sorrow.

He tried to affect a sneer as he approached, unable to just let her go and hold his silence. It was impossible not to feel something for her, though that something was far beyond words to describe it now. It wasn't that Vikram didn't know how he felt, it was just that he felt too many things at once.

"Bad" worked best as a descriptor. "Horrible" functioned even better.

"Why are you crying," he asked her, "did the miracle you were hoping for with Ashok not work out? Clearly you didn't feel it with me. Or did he dump you already? That's a record, even for him."

"Don't be awful, Vikram," Sahana muttered into her knees, "it doesn't suit you. I know you better than that."

"You know me better than most women," he said, "though I don't suppose that mattered to you at all. Was the taste of my lips that bad, that you couldn't wait to plant your lips on my best friend, of all people?"

"He's not your best friend," she told him. It was barely a whisper. "That man is no one's friend."

"Whatever," Vikram snarled, suddenly desperate for the scotch, "sit out here and freeze to death in the night for all I care. Or, even better--" he tossed the box of poetry at her feet, "use these to keep yourself warm. In this box are all the words I wasted on you. You can see the kind of man I was before I met you, sick, sad and alone. You can see the man who fell in love with you, the fool who sat there dreaming of you when you were dreaming of anybody but me. And you can see the man you have made me, furious and hard-hearted. Rest assured, I won't ever kiss anyone the way I kissed you, so you've taken that from me. My true love, my only dream. It's all yours now. Worthless as it is. Do with it what you will."

"Vikram, when Ashok kissed me--" Sahana's voice broke, and Vikram couldn't stand it.

"I don't care!" He shouted, kicking the box as he turned away from her. "Kiss whomever you want. I don't care."

117

"You do care," Sahana said, as fierce as he'd ever heard her. "You really think that I would hop on from one man to another? You really believe that I would kiss Ashok? Do you think so little of me?" Sahana wanted to slap the drunkenness out of Vikram but resisted.

Vikram just stared. His stomach felt sicker with every word she spoke.

"I didn't consent," Sahana continued, "to Ashok's touch, to his *kiss,*" she shuddered at the words. "He forced me against the wall and kissed me against my will. It was awful, and it hurt me. I escaped him, and I ran. I wanted to find you, I wasn't sure where to turn, but you were gone."

Vikram shook his head, unable to comprehend what he was hearing. Rage numbed his hearing to the point where her words were nearly inaudible. "Oh, Sahana," he said.

"He was drunk and horrible, and I thought he might hurt me." Sahana stressed, her voice rising and taking on a hysterical edge as she continued, "and I just wanted to find you and I didn't know where you were, and I needed you, and you weren't *there,* Vikram, you weren't--"

He took her in his arms without a second thought, holding her. With her in his arms, he realized that she was trembling. She smelled of fear, and her tears wouldn't stop coming. "Shh," he whispered into her hair, "I'm here now, I'm so sorry, I'm so sorry." There was nothing that he could say to make up for the awful words that had left his lips. How could he have blamed her; how could he have let his own jealousy put her into danger like this? What an awful, shallow man he was for letting his jealousy keep him from bringing her to safety.

And how evil was Ashok? Vikram had never heard of his friend behaving this brashly. Generally, Ashok thought of himself as a player, and he could be persistent, but to force himself on a woman, his equal, one deserving of respect and protection? It was so unlike him and so wicked that it made Vikram's blood run cold. He couldn't believe the words coming out of his mouth, even as he said them.

"I'll kill him," Vikram swore into Sahana's hair, "I'll destroy what he loves most, break his face until it's so hideous that no woman will look upon him again, I'll break his hands so that they can never touch you, I'll make sure he pays for what he's done--"

"Hush, Vikram," Sahana hissed back at him. "Don't talk like that. What's done is done, and I am safe here in your arms. Don't ruin your life as well as his by rushing at him in a fit of anger. Don't do something that would keep us apart forever. Think, regain your wits, and act like a gentleman. In this way you'll be able to exact the revenge you want and keep us both safe forever. I couldn't stand to lose you, not now, when I've just found you again."

"I can't stand the thought that he hurt you," Vikram spat back, and the taste in his mouth was bitter with anger and regret once more. No longer directed at Sahana, but at his so-called best friend, or the monster who had taken his place. "I can't stand the thought that he's just going to sleep it off in a comfortable bed while you won't be able to sleep a wink, knowing what he is, fearing him--"

Sahana kissed him to shut him up. And the feeling of her lips against his was so sweet and perfect. How could he have ever mistaken her for false? The woman was love incarnate.

There was nothing false about her. She had been his true love all along. When she pulled away she looked deeply into his eyes, the force of her words powerful enough to knock him back. "I fear nothing with you by my side," she said, "and I'll sleep well just so long as I am sleeping next to you. Don't let his rashness make you rash in return. Just stay here with me. That's the only revenge I need, to know that you are in my arms, and he cannot have me. It should be the only revenge you need as well. Breathe. Be with me. We'll figure out the rest when the sun rises."

"That's a long time from now," he told her. She tilted her head up to press a kiss to the edge of his jaw.

"Do you mind it? To lay with me here until morning? I —don't want to be alone tonight." Vikram couldn't agree more. He wanted to protect her and be with her – tonight and every night that followed. Also, he shuddered thinking of Ashok there in their dark cabin, reeking of Sahana's perfume and all the other sweetness he'd tried to take from her.

"Not at all," he told her, and her exhale released all the tension of this awful evening. It was over. All their fears and misunderstandings fell away, and it was just the two of them. The dance hall had long since gone silent and the people departed, unaware of the love that lay blooming in the grass right outside the door. If they had known, Vikram wondered, what would they have seen? A flower growing in the grass? A sunrise peeking out over the hill? What did their love look like to others?

To Ashok, it had looked like a threat. But Ashok himself had become a threatening thing. There was nothing that Vikram could do about it now. He needed to focus on Sahana. Sahana needed him.

Fourteen

The incessant thrumming of the train engine under their feet was a welcome rhythm, a dancing rhythm for Vikram's joyful heart. He could not keep the smile from his face, even though the train smelled of exhaust, and he could feel a hangover starting at his temples. He was the happiest person on the train, and his body sang with every mile they moved towards home. He was ready to go home. He had everything he needed with him. Even if he forgot his luggage, the one thing he cared about was in his arms. He was truly blessed.

On his arm, Sahana lay with her head pillowed against his shoulder, her breath coming in puffs as she slept. She breathed deeply, dreams he could not see swimming behind her eyelids. Her hand was in his, and it was the most precious thing he'd ever held. Her fingernails painted like rubies and two gold rings on her finger, he squeezed her hand and saw her smile in her sleep. He could only hope that she was dreaming of him. Thoughts of her were the only ones he could focus on.

No one on the train seemed to care where Sahana was sleeping. Hardly anyone seemed to notice at all except for Nalini, who flashed him a smile and a tentative thumbs-up. He returned the gesture as broadly as he could without waking Sahana up.

He had worried that gossip would overtake the whole office, with people asking how a woman like her could be with someone like him. After all, she was the sun, a rising star in Indian business, and the joy of their company since her transfer. Vikram was just a lowly assistant with little ambition and a sad, dreamy air to him that made him inaccessible. In fact, now that he was with her, people seemed downright friendly towards him. People from sales, who had barely spoken to him before except to ask off work, thumped him on the shoulder and smiled at him as they boarded the train. At first, he'd thought it was just the leftover sense of camaraderie from the retreat, but it felt now that Sahana was making him into a happier, friendlier person.

He should have known better than to worry that the office would be awash with gossip, mocking him and Sahana for their love. It was a new thing and people seemed content, or maybe they were too worried about their own lives and loves to say anything about his. So, he was left to his train seat and his little slice of heaven sleeping on his shoulder. The only bit of hell was the heat of Ashok's eyes beating into him as he glared.

He looked pale, sick, and lower than he usually was. That champion smile was dimmed and in its place was a snarl. It wasn't just jealousy or irritation, it felt like something akin to hate. It was hard to recognize on Ashok's face. It was even harder to recognize as it was directed towards him, coming from a man he'd thought was his friend. Vikram wanted to hate him back but couldn't work up the energy to feel hatred. In spite of everything that Ashok had done, the horror he'd inflicted upon Sahana and the pain he'd caused in pursuit of his own lust, Vikram couldn't work up the energy to feel anything more than apathy towards his old "friend." There was far too much love in his body for any real negativity to get through. He'd won Sahana's love. The approval of a friend who'd done nothing but hurt him for a long time wasn't of value to him anymore. Their relationship was over, in the past. Sahana was his future. She was the person who mattered most here.

Still, something about his actions made Vikram feel haunted in a way he couldn't explain. Ashok was never the one to let his face fall, to seem anything other than cheerful and light. He was in control of his emotions at all times. So, these uncharacteristic losses of control, these behaviors of violence and sexual rage, forcefulness and hatred, were unlike him. He was a planner, a plotter, a grand creator. He wasn't the sort of person who gave into impulse like this. The unpredictability of this new Ashok left Vikram feeling guarded. He wasn't certain how Ashok would retaliate, or if soon his smiling friend would return, blessing Sahana and Vikram's union with only a little bit of bitterness. Somehow, Vikram doubted that would happen. No matter how he wanted it to be true, he couldn't trust Ashok to be anything but an enemy from now on.

Deboarding the train was the easy part, even though he carried both his own luggage and Sahana's under his arms. She laughed, smacking his arm as he carried her things and insisting she was perfectly capable of managing without him. "After all, I've gotten this far, haven't I?" she asked him.

"But you see, my love, it's my job to make sure you never have to struggle again," he bowed, pretending to be gallant. Sahana giggled as she tried again to take her bags from his hands. He wasn't sure what she found funnier, the fact that he'd pretended to be her coachmen or the fact that he called her "love" in front of their friends.

Nalini rolled her eyes as she passed them. "You two," she said, but she was smiling. Her eyes were on her husband, politely waiting to take her bags from her, one of their small children balanced on his shoulders.

Vikram carried Sahana's bags all the way out the door, then all the way out to her car. Even once she'd opened the boot of her car, he didn't want to let go of them. She stood there looking at him, waiting expectantly. Then she laughed and he joined in. "I'm sorry," he said, "they're heavy but if I put them down, you'll go home, and I can't stand the thought of you leaving me."

"I was going to let you keep carrying them," she looked sheepish with one hand in her pocket as she grinned down at his shoes, "I'd walk all the way home if I were walking home with you. But then I'd have to leave you at the door, and I don't want to do that, either."

"Then don't," he said in a rush. His world was already tilted on its axis. Why not break the rules for love, live freely, and do what they wanted rather than worrying what people expected of them? Forget Ashok and the rest of the world, why not make one of their own? "Let's go back to my place. We can take your car. I just can't stand the thought of being without you. Not after we've just come together. I've been dreaming about you for so long, and I'm not willing to wake up just yet. Not without you in my arms."

"When you put it like that..." she hesitated for only a moment longer before her smile overtook her whole face, childlike with mischief and wonder. "Let's do it."

"Really?" he asked, just as excited as she was. The light in her soul was contagious. He could feel it from the inside out, glowing within him, changing him. The cobwebs of his sadness were washed away with every smile, every kiss.

"Absolutely," she said, dangling her car keys in front of him, "but it's my car, and I'm driving."

"I'm excellent at giving directions," he said, letting her luggage fall against his own in the boot of her car.

Like children they laughed and played in the car, turning up the radio and dancing all the way back to Vikram's house. Sometimes, while stuck in heavier traffic, he would hold her hand and she'd let him. It blew his mind every time that he wanted to touch her and she'd let him! Her hand was warm in his, and he felt his whole being drawn to the places where her fingertips touched his palm. Sahana was barely able to keep her eyes on the road. She had laughed out loud when he told her that if she didn't stop staring at him, she'd wreck the car before they could get back to his place.

"And that would be a shame," she said, "because there's so much I want to do to you once we get there."

"Drive faster," Vikram insisted, feeling warmth pooling in his belly at the thought of being alone with her, "but keep your eyes on the road."

Vikram felt self-conscious leading Sahana into the austere space of his apartment. It was a bachelor's apartment for certain. The walls were white and unpainted. There was no art hanging on them. His bookshelves were packed with books that were mostly unread and organized without rhyme or reason. The notebooks spilling from his shelves were dented and scratched-up, dog-eared, and sharpie-scribbled upon. There was laundry that had missed his hamper and a couple of dishes still left in the drying rack. It wasn't clean, but it wasn't lived-in either. It was an unused place of life and not a home.

"It's lovely," she commented, but he didn't have time to ask her if she meant it as they were kissing again. They moved faster this time, out of the view of prying eyes and in a place where they could finally be themselves. He wondered if he should suggest that they slow down. He wondered if he should tell her that they had all night. But the feeling of her in his arms was so incredible that he gave in without much of a struggle to her demanding kisses and the needy little noises she was making under her breath. Without the distraction of nature's beauty in this austere place, he could feel her touch more intensely than ever before. His body melted into hers, into the softness of her kiss and exploded with fireworks when his teeth scraped across her lips and she moaned, desperate pulling him closer. Their clothes seemed to fall like flower petals from their bodies as they backed into his bedroom, kissing all the way.

He pressed her onto the softness of his mattress, enjoying the way that the setting sun stained the white sheets pink and orange with dying light. The dim glow made her otherworldly somehow, more goddess than a woman. She smiled up at him, a hazy, sleepy smile as she strained upwards to beg another kiss from his lips. Another and another still, until finally, she pushed him off her, breathing hard.

"Get the condom," she told him, "I want more."

This wasn't the fast-paced desperation in the grass where he'd barely had time to tear open the condom and put it on before he was inside her. She watched with heavily lidded eyes as he dug through the drawer in his nightstand, grateful to every god that he had maintained enough optimism to keep a recent stash of condoms in spite of how little use he'd had for them before meeting Sahana.

"Go slowly," she told him as he tore open the wrapper, "I want to watch how you do it."

"Been a while?" he asked rhetorically, but she blushed down to her neck and couldn't meet his eyes.

"I'm new to this," she said, then took a breath, "by which I mean... when we first... that was my first."

Vikram blinked. "You're saying you were a..."

"Please don't be mad!" she said in a rush, "I'd been thinking about it for a while now, ever since I met you really--" Vikram nearly choked at the thought of that, Sahana, looking at him and wondering what it would be like to be with him. To be with any man. "All I wanted was you and you were wonderful. Everything I wanted in a man."

It all made sense now. Her desperation, her clumsy kisses. She said she'd never had time to date before coming to Chandigarh, and now here she was, with Vikram.

"It's alright," he told her. "I really don't mind. It's wonderful being with you, kissing you. If this is what you want, you can have it. If you want me. If you want to slow down, I'm okay with that, too. It's a lot to take in."

"I knew you'd be a gentleman about this. It's what I like about you. But I'm a grown woman, Vikram, and I know what I want," she said, pulling him closer. Her body against his was amazing. She knelt on the bed and kissed him, muttering against his lips, "now show me how to put on the condom, and the next time we do this, I'll put it on you."

Vikram was only too happy to comply.

Sliding into her body felt like coming home. Rocking against her made his nerves spark with every stroke. Each whimper and gasp, the way her fingernails scraped his back, filled him with a sense of desperation and urgency. Crashing into her body, relishing in the way she took him in and met him thrust for thrust, Vikram felt his breath coming in short gasps as she spasmed around him, letting out a moan that shook him to his core. The noises she made were more incredible now that he knew she was learning how to make them. He'd enjoyed her pleasure before but each touch was so powerful now, especially now that he knew he'd been the only man who had ever touched her like this, who had ever been inside of her. He took pride in each noise she made, knowing that he was the only person to hear her like this, to have her spread out before him, her body taking everything he gave her, and begging for more with each thrust.

This was heaven on earth. This was pure delight. Her body was the hottest place he'd ever been, and he could feel himself changing from the inside out as he drove into her again and again, feeling her convulse and tighten as she moaned in earnest, hands scrambling against his back, holding on for dear life. He'd been a man for a long time, but he'd never felt more like it than when they moved against each other in pure, ecstatic unison.

With one final sigh, his body exploded into pure pleasure, and he let her out from under him. They both lay there gasping heavily in the new darkness. There was no place their bodies weren't touching. Perfectly naked and safe under his bedsheets, Vikram took Sahana in his arms. He was never, never letting her go.

Fifteen

I n the morning, Vikram and Sahana bickered over who would cook breakfast, only to discover that neither one was particularly good at anything more difficult than pouring cereal into a bowl.

"Even then, I get the ratio wrong sometimes," Sahana confessed.

"Didn't your mother ever teach you how to cook?" Vikram asked, half laughing, swatting her on the behind with a kitchen towel as she scrubbed one of his pans clean.

"Didn't yours?" she retorted, "here, make yourself useful and dry up with that thing instead of wielding it like a weapon." With one last snap, which she artfully dodged, he did as she asked.

It was nice, working through a recipe together. Neither were cooks, but both were problem solvers by nature. "Two educated people trying to make an omelette. What could possibly go wrong?" He asked her, leaning over her shoulder to look at the screen of her phone. "College students cook omelettes. Children cook omelettes."

They burned the omelettes.

To be fair, they followed the recipe well enough. They made each measurement precisely and stirred their mixture to the consistency the recipe specified. They set the pan on medium and poured in the stirred ingredients with a delicate hand. It wasn't until after the omelette was in the pan that they lost themselves in each other's lips once more. The spell of love wasn't broken until suddenly Sahana sniffed the air.

"I smell burning," she said.

"Do you think it's time to flip it?" Vikram asked her.

"I think it's time to toss it in the trash and go out to eat," Sahana said, peering doubtfully through the smoke at the blackened omelette.

"Maybe it's supposed to look like that," Vikram said, desperate not to leave the house for some reason he could not understand. It was only when Sahana tilted her head back in laughter that his heart sang and he realized why he wanted her so close. This feeling, A beautiful woman in his apartment in no hurry to leave but in a hurry to kiss him more and more. What more could he want? With her by his side, he was happy, truly happy in a way he never had been before. All of the late nights spent dreaming of waking up to someone by his side, all the days spent lingering at the office rather than going home to an empty apartment. They were all leading up to this one perfect moment.

He pressed himself against her and kissed her deeply, there in the kitchen where smoke still wafting through their faces. She had morning breath, and her hair was tangled in knots. She hadn't bothered to touch up her makeup, knowing that he would just get it messy again. Barefoot and utterly human, disheveled but smiling as brilliantly as a diamond, he was more in love with her than he'd ever been before.

"Come on," he said finally, pulling away, "I'll buy you breakfast. We've got to keep your strength up. There are so many things I want to show you today."

She strained up to take another kiss from his lips. He smiled, squeezing her hand as she turned towards the bathroom, "I've got to freshen up," she said, "and then I actually do have to go back into the office for just a little bit."

Vikram groaned, "no, no office, not today. You've been granted this one day off, use it."

"The day off is for other people, Vikram. People like you. I'm the head of an entire department, and as hard as I've tried to get the world to stop, it hasn't yet. This trip was really just supposed to be an inconvenience. I was dreading it at first," Sahana smiled, her face soft and open, "but then, there was you. You made everything better, and you'll make today better, too. I'll come home to you as soon as I can finish my work."

"Will that be before six this evening?" he asked her, "It's spoiling the surprise, I know, but there's a poetry open mic that I go to Monday nights after work, and I was wondering if you'd be able to make it?"

She poked her head out of the bathroom and stopped him in his tracks. It was amazing-- she still managed to take his breath away even now, with toothpaste dribbling down her chin, "Oh, definitely. I'll be back before you know it. I just need to make a couple of phone calls and meet with a client.

I should be back right after five. And I've got plenty of time for breakfast right now."

"Then let's not waste any more time," he said with a grin, following her into the bathroom to run a washcloth across his face and strip the smell of sex from his skin.

They finally made their way down to a restaurant that was nearly deserted at the late hour of the morning. There they could sit and talk to their heart's content without worry of being mocked for their new blossoming love. The only person mocking Vikram was Sahana, who stared just as hard at him as he watched her eat.

"What?" she asked him, "is their *chutney* on my face?"

"No," he said, "you're just beautiful."

In his apartment parking lot, they parted ways with a long, slow kiss. "Sure I couldn't convince you to come upstairs for a glass of water?" he asked, "it's awfully hot out here."

"Don't think I don't know your game, mister," she said, pushing at his chest with one manicured hand, "if I go back up there, I'll never leave. I'll see you at the poetry reading tonight."

One more kiss, long and lingering, but not enough to last forever. Then she was gone. He hated to see her leave. The only thing he was looking forward to was the inside of his notebook. There he could see her anytime, examine the minute details on her skin, and the flecks of gold in her irises. There he'd stay until it was time to meet her at the coffee shop.

His phone buzzed with an incoming text.

Remember-- turmeric latte, no whipped cream! XO

He smiled, pocketing his phone as he took the steps back up to his apartment two at a time.

At the coffee shop, the first thing he did was sign up for the open mic. The second thing he did was order her drink. He'd arrived a few minutes before he told her to meet him just in case the open mic list filled up too fast and denied him a chance to perform. So, he was expecting to see her walk through the door soon. She hadn't texted him to let him know that she was on her way, but he knew from experience how draining it could be to have to go into the office. She'd probably just forgotten in her race to get back to him.

He settled down at a table for two and pulled out his notebook, reading over the poem that he wrote in order to feel it in his mouth. Something lovely on the page might sound clumsy when read aloud. It was a fact he'd learned the hard way when he was still a novice at this particular open mic. Luckily the people had been so kind and supportive that he'd kept coming back. He loved this coffee house. It had shaped him as a poet like few things ever had.

It was hard to focus on his notebook when his eyes kept darting to the door, pleasant anticipation fluttering in his stomach as he watched for her familiar walk, the way that her hair would shine under the dim lights of the coffee shop. His own coffee was bitter and bold, a simple dark roast. He was glad he hadn't put any whipped cream into her drink. It would have melted into the latte by now.

As the MC for the open mic opened up the evening, Vikram shot off a quick, nervous text to Sahana. The room was getting packed and would only fill further as the night went on. The churning crowd of people might hide even

Sahana's beauty from him. Finding her would be impossible if she didn't get here soon.

Third table to the left from the counter. Can't wait to see you! :)

He received no reply. His coffee was drained to the dregs, and two poets had already read their work. They were talented, and on any other night he would have enjoyed their work immensely, but now, he could only worry. So many bad scenarios flashed across his mind. A car wreck. A mugging outside of work gone wrong and leaving her bleeding on the pavement while his text messages flashed across her screen, blissfully unaware of the tragedy that had just occurred. She'd promised she'd be here. She felt the same pull towards him that he felt towards her. Why wasn't she here with him? Why wasn't she answering her phone?

You okay?

He sent off, just as the MC leaned into the microphone and said, "Now presenting a perennial favorite: Vikram Shan!"

There was scattered applause as Vikram made his way to the stage, aware that his palms were sweaty with worry. It was hard to focus on reading, but there was no backing out now. Besides, maybe Sahana's phone was off. Maybe she was in the crowd looking for him and would hear his words like he wanted her to hear them.

> *the birds don't change their tune*
> *the river flows on its same path*
> *the rain falls as it always does*
> *omelettes burn and toothpaste*
> *dribbles its way down your chin*

work waits for us, traffic stands still
dump the trash and tend the garden
order takeout and call your mother
do the small, important acts life requires
like the diligent lover you are
love doesn't change the world
when you become aware of it
love has been the world all along.

The applause in the small room was deafening, a sea of noise and dim lights as people whistled and cheered enough to get him off the stage and onto the next poet. A couple of people he vaguely knew clapped him on the back. He could barely feel their applause and admiration. What he could feel was the gaping absence of Sahana in the room. He'd wanted her to be there. But she wasn't there. He was all alone in this crowded room.

Her phone went straight to voicemail when he called. Without another moment's thought, Vikram hailed a cab to where she'd last said she'd be: the office. At this late hour, he didn't expect anyone to be there, but if something horrible had happened, it would have had to happen there. He'd find her. Whatever happened, he'd make sure she was safe. She wouldn't have just abandoned him for no reason. Something had happened. He'd start at the beginning and find out what.

By the time the cab pulled in front of the office, Vikram had steeled his nerves. He knew he had to soon face Ashok for what he forced Sahana to endure, but that was a conversation for another day. He also knew he would have to explain everything to Mr. Patil as well, but he pushed that thought too from his mind. Right now, his focus was Sahana, and he was dead worried as to why she was not responding.

Sahana's smiling face flashed in front of his eyes as he slid his key card and made his way towards the marketing floor. All the lights were off and no one was there, not even Nalini. Everyone had gone home. Sahana's office was locked tight, and she was not there. His mind swam. Perhaps there had been a wreck after all. Perhaps something bad truly had happened to her, and what he'd thought was an anxious imagination was really some sixth sense. Clearly, she hadn't been caught up at work like he'd first excused. His anxieties sharpened into knives in his guts, stabbing him as he nearly raced to his desk to see if she had left him a note explaining her whereabouts.

In the sales department, it was almost as deserted. There was nothing out of place on his desk to indicate that she had stopped by at all, but there was a light on in Ashok's office. Vikram could feel his heart in his throat as he realized that Ashok was still inside, sitting at his desk.

Vikram, now desperate about Sahana's whereabouts, decided to see Ashok. If Sahana was in today for work, then maybe Ashok had seen her. Maybe he could shed some light as to events of today. Though he wanted to confront Ashok and force his former friend to see some sense, he wanted to tell him that his actions were unacceptable, but he decided otherwise.

He opened the door controlling his wrath only to see that Ashok was bleary-eyed and beyond drunk. Nearly wasted. His tie was undone, and he had a regretful expression on his sloppy face as he stared deeply into his tumbler of scotch, frowning and thinking thoughts so deep that Vikram thought at first his old friend had not noticed him come in.

But Ashok did notice him after what felt like a long moment, pulling his gaze away from the tumbler of scotch and locking his dark eyes with Vikram's. His features sharpened into a pointy grin, shark-like, when he realized who it was in front of him. Vikram immediately felt his hackles raised, terrified of this man sitting in front of him, who he no longer recognized at all.

"Ah, Vikram," he slurred, just as Vikram opened his mouth to speak, "I was hoping you'd come in today after hours, and not tomorrow. It's for the best, really. You were my friend, after all, and doing this will be far more humiliating in front of an office full of your friends and coworkers. Sit down, have one last drink with me before you pack up your desk. You're fired."

Sixteen

Cold shock blossomed in Vikram's gut as he took in the words Ashok had just said. "You're fired."

Vikram had never been fired before, had never given anyone a reason to do so. He was competent, kind, and eager enough to help, even when the work didn't consume or interest him, and he had other things he'd rather do. He'd never given anyone reason to report or demote him, never done lazy or slapdash work. There was no reason he'd be fired. Especially not after a long weekend during which Mr. Patil had done nothing but celebrate Vikram's hard work and thank him for his service to the company.

"I hate your sense of humor," Vikram said flatly, "especially when you're drunk." His hands flexed with the effort to keep his fists from clenching. He tried to keep his posture easy and open as Ashok poured him a drink. He didn't want to sip it. He was done pretending that they were best of friends. They were this close to going to war.

"This isn't a joke," Ashok told Vikram as he sat back down in his seat, templing his fingers, "you're fired. This shouldn't come as a surprise to you."

"This comes as a total surprise to me, Ashok," Vikram said slowly, trying to process the storm cloud of feelings inside him. Rage was overcoming shock at this point, indignation piled on top of shock, piled on top of worry for Sahana. He didn't want to be sitting here, listening to Ashok's nonsense. He had far more pressing worries than the state of his own job. Sahana was missing, and he had no idea where she was. "I've been nothing but good to you, even when you've been horrid to me. That's the foundation of our friendship, isn't it?"

"Don't play dumb," Ashok snapped. He was acting like an authoritarian but came off as more of a monster. When he was furious his broad shoulders seemed hulking and massive. Vikram imagined just how afraid Sahana must have been, pinned by such a massive man. It filled him with righteous fury. "I'm afraid it's our friendship that has allowed me to overlook your flaws for too long. I was blind to your behavior, and now I see the truth."

"I feel like that's my line," Vikram snapped, "I feel like you're taking the words directly out of my mouth. Are you sure this isn't some sick joke?"

"Sexual assault is no laughing matter." Ashok slammed his hand on the desk. The noise made Vikram jump.

Vikram narrowed his eyes, refusing to back down. Ashok was unpredictable and untrustworthy, but Vikram wouldn't surrender. "On that, we are in perfect agreement. You'd know all about sexual harassment, given what you did to Sahana."

He didn't expect Ashok's laugh, a short, disappointed bark that held no humor. "What I did?" he asked, disbelieving, "No, Vikram, your actions are your own. Shoulder them like a man and take responsibility for them."

Vikram's brows knit in confusion for only a second before it all clicked into place. He didn't want to believe it but it was all coming together. There was only one logical conclusion: he was being framed. That was why Ashok was keeping up this pretense. He was saving his own skin, knowing that after assaulting Sahana, the only way he'd be able to save himself from the scandal was to create a bigger scandal.

It was as though the blood drained out of his head. He felt woozy for a moment, seeing stars as the gravity of the situation sunk through him, pinning him to the chair he was sitting in. He wanted to stand up and walk away. He wanted to flip the desk in front of him. Instead, he could only stare as Ashok unraveled his world.

"The whole office knows," Ashok said, spelling it out slowly, as though he were relishing how the confession tasted in his mouth. They were bitter in Vikram's ears. "Sahana knows."

"What does she know?" he shot back, aware that with every word, he was fighting for his life. If Ashok framed him for this, he'd never work again. The claim seemed ludicrous, but Ashok was a smart man. He wouldn't start a fight he didn't believe he could finish. Vikram would have to give his all if he wanted to survive. "She knows about you pinning her against the wall, trying to kiss her. She knows that you threatened her, assaulted her, and wouldn't take no for an answer. She knows you're unpredictable, that you assaulted her. She knows the truth that will lose you your job," Vikram spoke with venom.

"But that's nothing-- nothing! Compared to what she knows you did to her now," Ashok barked. "What I did was a misunderstanding, crossed wires. What you did was all out betrayal of someone you claimed to love." He sounded gleeful, leaning over his tumbler of scotch. "You humiliated her. The whole office knows everything the two of you did together. It's a wonder you even showed your face after what you said to everyone. Did you really think Sahana wouldn't find out?"

Vikram blinked. It was as though he'd tripped through a mirror and found their situations reversed. He wasn't sure what to say. He couldn't believe his own ears.

"Sahana will know the truth, in the end," Vikram stammered, "Whatever it is you've made up--"

"You told people such sordid details about your relationship. Or should I say, your *relations*." Ashok hissed the word, a gleeful sneer across his lips, "It seemed like a pretty carnal relationship, the way you bragged about your own stamina, about the easy way she gave into you. On the lawn of the campground, in the showers of her cabin! You had no decency when you revealed to people exactly what you'd done to her. She was humiliated by details only the two of you could have known. I won't repeat what you said, out of respect for her. She's a lady, no matter how you tried to frame her."

"How could anyone know the details of what we shared?" Vikram almost whispered, his shock turning to horror. To have such a beautiful night repeated back to him so sordidly disgusted him. He felt nauseated by the words coming out of Ashok's mouth.

"Indeed," Ashok agreed too easily, his smirk darkening, "Really, it's not as though anyone else was there to see you. Only you could have spread such filthy rumors to the whole office. You told your best buddy, and from there, the rumor spread. It was only when he realized just how far you'd taken your bragging that he had to go to his superiors and turn you in. Isn't that right?"

Too late, Vikram realized what had happened. This wasn't just a betrayal on Ashok's part. This was a plot that he'd hatched to save his own skin and throw Vikram under the bus. Vikram felt sick, his skin crawling as he realized that the most magical moment of his life, when he and Sahana first united, had been observed by a worm like Ashok. He hadn't revealed any of the details of their encounter to anyone. He'd even been tight-lipped around Nalini, a friend who he trusted. He couldn't stand the thought that people would believe he was so sadistic towards a woman he loved.

"-- and I can understand why you'd want to brag. A loser like you graced with the love of a goddess like Sahana? Any beautiful woman in your bed when it's been empty for so long, I can see why you'd want the world to know." Ashok chuckled dryly, "But this is a workplace, Vikram. Sahana is your superior. And for you to disrespect her, not just as a fellow coworker but as a woman, is so hideous. I've already sent an email to Mr. Patil outlining your unacceptable behavior. I know that others will corroborate my report. You've humiliated your fellow employee, and humiliated yourself in the process."

"It's you," Vikram felt a fire burning in his chest. This went beyond the protective sensation he'd had when he realized how Ashok had tormented Sahana the first time. To injure her so badly, to use what had been a beautiful night, and ruin and wreck all their good memories together and to make her seem like a common whore to the whole office-- it couldn't be forgiven. "You saw us, you're the source of this rumor. Sahana will know the truth, and Mr. Patil will know what it is you've done. I would never, ever torture her like that. You're the one who assaulted her. She's probably frightened of you now, but I'll make sure that the truth is found out and she never has to fear you again."

It was only Sahana's voice in his head that kept him from striking Ashok on the spot. He remembered her saying that violence would solve nothing, and to get revenge the right way, through proper channels. He regretted that he hadn't struck Ashok on the spot or yelled to the whole office about Ashok's betrayal of Sahana when he'd had the chance back at the retreat. The time he'd given Ashok was enough for the cunning man to formulate this dastardly plan to save his own skin.

Now Vikram was under examination, and if he struck out at Ashok now, he would look like a disgruntled employee trying to exact clumsy revenge. If he wanted to fight for his life, he'd have to be smarter. He'd have to fight with his mind and not his fists.

Vikram knew that if he kept his cool, he'd be able to clear his name. But it would depend on whether or not Sahana would speak to him again. After the carnage that Ashok had wrought on their tender new relationship, Vikram knew that to ever get her to trust him again would take time. And time was something he was in short supply of.

"She'll never believe it," Vikram told him with a confidence he did not entirely feel, "even with what you know, there's more that you'll never know. The love we share, our feelings for each other. You know nothing of love."

"Love?" Ashok scoffed, looking down at Vikram. Vikram bristled with fury, knowing that in reality, Ashok had hated him for years and was just starting to act upon it now. "What a foolish romantic you are, even until the end. Love doesn't make a woman leave the office with tears streaming down her cheeks. Love doesn't humiliate the way you've humiliated her. It's one thing to kiss and tell, but Sahana was a lady. And to spread to everyone that she was a virgin before you, to brag about having taken that? Poor Sahana, she thought you were special. She thought she could trust you with something she'd never shared with anyone else before. I don't know that she'll recover from everything you did."

Vikram's blood turned to ice. "How did you know?" It was barely a whisper in his mouth. The shock within him made him feel a million kilometers away from the conversation. How come Ashok knew about it? That conversation had taken place that morning between Sahana and himself in the privacy of his home while no one was around to hear.

"That she was a virgin?" Ashok chuckled, "I know because you spread a rumor that's reached the entire office. How did you know? Well, you said yourself, the way she was flopping around on top of you like an eel, clumsy and unpracticed, it was obvious to anyone who's been around the block once or twice what it looks like when a virgin gives it up--"

"Stop," Vikram hissed, "stop speaking about her with such repulsive disrespect."

"I'm quoting you, oh poet," Ashok mocked.

"I'd never say such a thing! I'd never reveal such a thing. Especially not in such a crass, disgusting way," he blustered, almost losing his temper completely. His fist itched for contact with Ashok's smug face. He wanted to break, to bruise, to force onto Ashok all the agony that he'd given to Sahana and himself. But he couldn't get angry, not now, not with so much at stake.

He collected himself again with a deep breath, taking a long sip from his drink. The scotch burned his mouth but quenched the fire within him long enough to collect his thoughts. "Ashok-- I'm not you. This will be your undoing. You can try and frame me to save yourself after the mistake you've made, but in the end, I'll make sure it costs you everything."

Ashok laughed again. Vikram wished he could smack the smug look off of his former friend's face. "Vikram, don't you see it? I've already won. Enjoy your drink. It will be your last on the company's dime. I'm ashamed that I ever hired such a desperate, jealous, sad little man. It seems that I was right all along about your true worth. You're nothing, Vikram, and you'll never be anything more."

"I'm far more in Sahana's eyes," Vikram insisted. Ashok rolled his eyes. "And even if she leaves me and never speaks to me again, she'll never forgive you. She'll make sure that if I go down, you go down with me."

"Sahana misjudged you, Vikram," Ashok explained, patiently as though he were talking to a dim child, "and now she thinks she's misjudged everything. She's broken and ashamed by the things you have said. She'll never say a word about me. She'll forget my small injury in the sea of wounds you've unleashed upon her. And given time to think and reflect, she'll see that I had her best interests at heart all along. The damage you've done to her heart will, in the end, harden it. And I will ensure she softens towards me. I'll have her in the end. I'll have everything I need and leave you with nothing."

"Why are you doing this?" Vikram asked, nearly a plea, trying to reach whatever part of their friendship still lived in Ashok. Ashok's response made it clear that friendship had died forever. Vikram felt no mourning at the knowledge. All he felt was rage.

"It had to be done, so I might as well take pleasure in it," Ashok said with a shrug. "She really was the perfect girl for you, but I wanted her more. If you hadn't held on so hard, I wouldn't have had to ruin your life. But in the end, if it gets me what I want, you only live once, and I want it all. Pity you had to get in the way."

"I'm not packing up my things," Vikram replied, "I'm not going down without a fight."

Ashok laughed. "Do as you wish. Come into the office tomorrow shouting about a conspiracy. Stalk Sahana to the ends of the earth if it makes you happy. Punch me and throw a temper tantrum like a child, but in the end, it will change nothing. I told you before Vikram, you lost, and I've meant it. The game I've been playing all along is rigged for my success.

I'm sorry, old friend, that you were standing in my way. But it's over now. And nothing you do will change that."

Vikram snarled. "We'll see about that, 'old friend.' What you don't know is the way this world works. It runs on love. And cynical plotting fools like yourself never win, even when you seem to have the upper hand." And with that warning, he walked out, determined to make things right. The office shook with the force of his slamming the door.

Seventeen

His phone was as useless as a brick in his pocket. He knew Sahana wouldn't call. He knew he shouldn't call her. He could only ignore the emails from work flooding into his inbox through the evening, including one from Nalini that was full of such unexpected venom over what horrible things he had 'done' that it made his hands quiver with shame and fear. He wanted to call his dear friend and explain just what Ashok had done, but he didn't dare. Time would come when he would discuss everything with Nalini, but first, he would speak to Mr. Patil or Sahana herself. He would fight this battle with integrity and his head held high. He deserved that. Sahana deserved it.

He wanted to call her, to speak to her, to see her face. Even with the horror that Ashok had wrought in their newly budded relationships, he wanted her. His heart hadn't gotten the message that his mind already knew: that she didn't want to see him. He couldn't help but crave her, and knowing that he couldn't have her made him feel like giving up, crawling into bed, and never getting out again. He missed her more than anyone else on the earth. Without her, he was lonely. He thought of her smile and what he'd give to see it again. He'd give this useless job, all his dreams, and all his plans. He'd give anything he had, break his fingers so he'd never write again. He'd do anything to see her again, looking at him with love in her heart and that sunshine smile on her lips.

The only respectful option to see her again would be to wait until the next time they were at work. And then he knew her expression would be that of pain and sorrow, not of love. He'd shoulder the sting of that look just to see her heart happy once more. He dressed slowly in the morning, trying to figure out what to wear. He wasn't sure what to eat. Everything in his life felt uncertain, fraught with peril. And then the fear of swiping his keycard, for the first time not knowing whether or not it would work. If security would meet him on his walk up the stairs and force him back out onto the street. His biggest fear was standing at the door to the marketing department. He knew he shouldn't enter. He knew he shouldn't approach her. But what else could he do? Sahana was his saving grace. His only shot at surviving this horror.

It was only her in the office. And how beautiful she was, haloed in the morning light that filtered through the office window. It reminded him of their last morning together, before everything went so wrong. He could have stared at her all day, safe in the warm feeling of reminiscing. But then she saw him.

The look on her face was sharper than any blade and he felt it in his ribs, a sharp ache that threatened to bring him falling onto his knees. She shut the door to her office as he approached, not even allowing him to get a word out.

His hand hovered above the door, almost too afraid to knock. He gathered himself, reminded himself of his innocence, and knocked, once.

"Go away Vikram, or I'll call security." Her voice sounded hollow, broken. He wanted to kill Ashok for what he'd done to Sahana. He wanted to break down the door between them and hold her until she had no more questions about whether or not she was the love of his life, someone he adored too much to disrespect in the way she'd been disrespected. But this wasn't a fairy tale. This was real life, and their pain lasted long after the book was closed on their story.

"Sahana, please," he pleaded, "you know me. You know my respect for you, how I adore you. Awful lies have been spread about you, but I was not the source of those rumors."

Sahana cracked the door just a millimeter. He did not try to push her any farther. "That's the thing, Vikram. They weren't lies. They were just filthy, crass versions of the truth," she spoke in a harsh tone. "I thought you were a poet. To hear what I thought was our love story spread in snickers throughout the halls, by people who weren't even on the retreat-- acquisitions and payroll both had hideous things to say-- I'm disgusted. I'm heartbroken. But it had to be you. You are the only person who knew the truth about me, about what happened between us. The details you shared, filthy as they were, are true. Offer me this respect, at least: take responsibility for your actions."

"They were Ashok's, not mine!" Vikram insisted, trying not to raise his voice. He should have known better than to hope that Sahana would believe his innocence. After all, Ashok had committed nearly the perfect crime in spreading that rumor. It was a hard web to untangle, one that he'd only been able to weave because he knew Vikram so well. "He followed us. He watched us. About your virginity, I won't say how he guessed because what he said to me was repulsive. But he almost as good as admitted that he'd spread the rumor."

Sahana shifted inside her office but the door remained mostly shut. He heard her sigh. "You two are always using each other as a convenient excuse. I couldn't because Ashok did this. I never learned because Vikram did that. You're both as bad as each other. You would have to be, to have been his friend. I don't know why I didn't see it from the start."

"You were right," he told Sahana, a vehement plea. He could feel tears welling in his eyes as he begged her to understand, "he was never my friend. And I'm sorry that I clung to something that wasn't real, trusting him as long as I did. I never knew that he'd be capable of such treachery, though he'd always seemed capable of it. I was a fool who thought our friendship was special and good. Instead, it was a poison I held inside so long that now I fear it may kill me."

"It's killed me as well, Vikram. How do you think I can show my face around here? I'm hiding my head in shame, trying to come to work as early as I can and leave when no one is watching. I'm ashamed, though my only fault was loving you. I had been so stupid and unwise. I won't recover from it. I've requested a transfer back home. I'll be demoted even though this job is all I've ever wanted, but it will be worth it not to have to be around horrible men like you and Ashok."

"You can't leave," Vikram protested, the thought of it making his blood run cold. Just how much was Ashok willing to ruin to save his own skin? Clearly, more than he'd ever thought possible. He hated that Sahana had called him horrible, but he had to prove to her he wasn't. He had to prove his true love. He'd do whatever it took to make sure she knew without a doubt that he was devoted to her. Whether they were together or not.

"I can do as I please," she shot back, and Vikram corrected himself.

"No," he reiterated, "You can do as you please, but this isn't what you want to do. You just got here. You just started building a life. You just started making friends. This was supposed to be your crowning glory, not your shame!"

"Look at what you've turned it into!" Sahana shouted, "look at what's happened to me!"

Vikram shouted back, desperate to keep her from shutting the door, "I won't let your life be ruined because of Ashok's treacherous plan. He's doing everything he can to save his own skin, trying to run us both off because we know that he assaulted you. But if we condemn him, we'll both save our own reputations and save our workplace from a predator in the process. It's the only way."

"You won't win me back with this," Sahana snapped, but the door opened just a hair more. "I'm not a prize to be won. I'm a woman, the one you've damaged. Gallant showmanship is the stuff of fairytales. We live in the real world. You don't get to save the world and win the girl."

"I'm not asking for you to come back to me," Vikram agreed, though his heart broke to say it. "If things are over between us, if the sight of me disgusts you, I don't mind to find a new job, to never see you again. Even though I feel like it might kill me. I think you're it for me. I think you're the only shot at true love I've ever had. But I'm willing to give that up just to see you happy, if that's what you truly desire."

"I don't know what I truly desire," Sahana said, and her hand crept through the crack in the door. Vikram took it in his, and she did not pull away. "I want this not to have happened. I desire my reputation, my friends, you. I desire not to feel this way. Can you make that happen, gallant prince?"

"I'm not sure," he answered honestly, "like you said, it's not a fairytale. But I can promise you this: I'm fighting for you, not just to save myself. I'll hold your best interests at heart and do the best I can for you. At the end of the day, if you decide I'm not in your best interests, I'll back off without a fight. I'll never force you or try to conquer you. I'll only love you."

"And what if love isn't enough?" she asked, and he could hear her heart breaking in her voice. He wanted to slide through the door and into her waiting arms, to hold her and comfort her the way only a soulmate could.

"If love isn't enough, we'll find something else on which to survive. I'll be there for you, loyal and true, whatever you decide. But don't ruin your career and future because of a shark like Ashok. Those who are wicked won't prevail-- they can't." His own vehemence surprised him, but he was nearly shouting once he finished his sentence. How dare this happened to them? How dare anyone got in the way of their happily ever after together? Just who did Ashok think he was to stand in the way of love?

"This isn't a story, Vikram--" she protested, and he squeezed her hand.

"But it is. It's our love story. And I believe that in our love story, the good will win and the bad will fail. Because it's you and me. It's what we know to be right. So, it has to be the ending."

"I love you," she said, a sob escaping from her lips as she withdrew her hand from his, "even now, with all these hardships. Even then, with those horrible things I thought you'd said about me, I loved you. As much as I hated myself for it. As much as I thought it would kill me. But I have to think. I can't just take this as the truth and fall into your arms. Even though I want to be weak and do just that."

"Then think," he said, even though his heart ached to hold her in his arms. He had to be brave and let her take her time in coming back to him. His heart was heavy with the real possibility that she wouldn't, that she'd been injured too badly to love anyone again, much less him. But he had to have faith in her mind, in her heart, in their love. In spite of the ache in his own heart, he had to give her the space to heal from the pain Ashok had inflicted. So he told her, "I'm going to go home. There's nothing more I can do here, and if I see Ashok, I might be moved to inflict pain on him myself. I just had to see you, to see if there was anything I could do to heal the hurt in your heart. That's all I want in the end. I want to do everything I can to soothe your pain."

"This is something I have to do for myself," she told him, stuttering a little. He still hadn't seen her face, and he missed it terribly. He didn't dare ask to see her, "but thank you for trying. For loving me. I'll-- I'll see you again soon. We'll talk again soon. Go home. I'm sure you'll be receiving a call from Mr. Patil that will summon you back here soon enough."

"I'm sure," he said, still to the door. "And I'll be there when he does. Not for my own sake, but for yours."

"Go," she said, "get some rest. This isn't over yet. We aren't over yet. We're just--" she paused, sighing again.

"Getting to our happily after," he said. The door clicked shut behind him as he made his way out of the office. His heart was still broken, but he could feel the uncomfortable itch of healing beginning in its deepest wounds. They would survive this. He just had to have faith.

Eighteen

The ground underneath Vikram felt as delicate as a rose petal under his feet. Every step he took up the stairs to his apartment felt as though the ground might give way underneath him. His head felt woozy. So much stress and excitement and fear and love lived within him. The weight of all his thoughts and feelings made him sick. His feet were like concrete. His stomach was like lead. If being with Sahana was like flying, being without her was like being crushed under the weight of too much gravity.

He hated his brain, so human, so full of fear. He hated the constant looping of his worried thoughts. He wanted to get them out on paper, but the thought of even writing one down scared him. To write was to make real. He didn't want any of this to be happening. So, he lay on the couch and shivered. The uncertainty of his world frightened him. The love he'd spent his whole life dreaming about had never come paired with so much heartache. He'd experienced boredom, betrayal, but never the threat of losing something precious. He'd never had anything truly precious to lose. His heart was willing to be shattered if doing so would save Sahana's from cracking further.

That was the terrifying thing about love: until you had it, you didn't know its true worth. You knew that it was something worth having, something worth dying for, something strong enough on which to build a life, but the true measure of its worth remains elusive to all but those who loved.

Vikram tried to go through his regular routine. Microwaved roti for supper, ate it on the couch as he stared at his television screen. But still, he managed to lose himself in a daydream anyways, his eyes flickering as he remembered one perfect moment of Sahana's kiss and the next moment the snick of the door shutting as she told him to leave her be. He couldn't bear it. And yet still, his breath came and his heart beat in his chest. Even without her by his side. He was living without her to sustain him. He'd done it most days of his life. But what only one month ago had been his reality now seemed impossible. He wasn't sure how to be without her.

One breath at a time, he reminded himself as he felt the air in his lungs begin to sting. Each breath took him closer to resolution. Either she would love him or she would not, but his breaths would carry him there and far beyond. His breath would take him through the rest of his life.

This love was unreasonable. He felt parched, mouth cracking, and blood on his tongue every time he imagined living life without her. He lay on his couch. He stared at the ceiling listening to his upstairs neighbors walking across their floorboards and his downstairs neighbors playing a love song that seeped through the thin walls. Was he the only person in this whole apartment complex who lived alone?

He craved her. He dreamed. He fell into a fitful sleep in which he chased her as though they were children, through a garden made of gauzy paper, never sure if he was trapped by curtains that held back the light or bandages that stopped bleeding. He found her and lost her and found her again, over one thousand different lifetimes and behind one thousand shimmering veils that stuck to his skin like spiderwebs. Suddenly, he was drowning, pinned by her gaze. She stood above him, as high as the stars in the sky, just as cold and out of reach as they were to Vikram there on earth.

"What a fool," she told him pityingly, swimming before him wrapped in blue silk. Each word she said blew like a bubble from her mouth, popping against his face. It was all the oxygen he could find so deep underwater, even though it stung like a wasp to hear her words, "What a fool. To worship love when so many other gods exist. Money and power, greed and jealousy, all have so much hold on this earth. But love, such a meek thing, so weak and quiet. A pauper's god. One that takes and takes."

She spoke, and her words increased in volume until they were shaking through him like a wall of sound. Above him the sky rippled like it had been bombed, tearing through all the silk and water until it fell like shredded tissue paper at his feet. Another ripple of her voice shook across the water, stirring them until they cocooned him, brushing across his face as she whispered, "what a fool, to see love everywhere and think you could ever truly possess it. That it could ever truly be yours."

The blue silk turned blood red and the water around her murky, obscuring her face until it was no longer hers at all, but instead Ashok's. His expression was thick and ugly and twisted with rage. There was no oxygen in the words he said. Vikram was suffocating in them. "Love makes a martyr of you. You'll always die for someone else's mistakes when love is the God you worship."

"We're all going to die for something," Vikram managed to choke out even though the water was thick as glue and stuck between his teeth, trying to silence even the whisper of his breath, "I'd rather die for her than die alone in foolish pursuit of money."

"Love will never make you happy," Ashok's voice echoed in his ears.

"A broken heart can heal," he countered, and he knew it now to be true as the words left his lips, "but one that has never known love, one that's cold and merciless, that's a heart that will never be fixed."

"You are the man I want," it was Sahana's voice again crashing around him like a brilliant dawn. Suddenly Vikram was on dry land, gasping into the sand of a riverbank while she sparkled above him, just as radiant as the sun. Her voice rang out like a note pulled from a crystal glass. Her eyes were hot as melted honey on his face. She sounded like forgiveness. "You are a man I could love." With that, the whole world bloomed into brilliant, perfect morning, and the face of the sun dropped down to envelop him in a perfect, eternal kiss.

Vikram blinked at his ceiling, awaked in the darkness by his own beating heart. He was scrambling to find a pen before he had even blinked the sleep from his eyes. This scribbling was not for a notebook, but for a sheet of letter paper. It was meant not to be shared with the whole world, but with the one person for whom his world turned. He kept his handwriting neat, his words simple, and his message as true to his heart as he could possibly hope to reflect. From his pen spilled more confidence than he had felt in days. His fate was set. His course was straight. There was only one thing he needed to ask her to do.

Sahana,

The role of the optimist is a hard role to play, but still, I do my best to smile and look towards our uncertain future as though it were a weather forecast predicting a week of sunny skies. How can I not? I only know one way to love, and that is the way in which you have taught me. With a smile on my face and a song in my heart, a pretty little tune that wraps around the vowels of your name and keeps time to the blood pulsing in my veins. This love is visceral, all-consuming. And yet my soul feels as light as air under its heavy burden. I can do nothing but love you. It feels better, even now with the sting of all the hurt between us. I want nothing more than to be with you. I am designed to be yours, and I long for our union. Bring me back to where I belong. Hold me tight against you once more.

I am writing not to beg but to plead my case. I know it is bold, more forward than I was even at your office door, but I am resolute. I know what I want. And I have decided you ought to love me anyway. In spite of all the world between us and what has happened, I think we can live together in the soft light of morning, putting to rest all the nightmares we have lived. We will overcome them. They will fade away. In the face of true love all things unworthy must wither, and all things good and true will be nourished. So, hold on for that morning, where we are together. That light is worth fighting for.

I'm asking you to do something bold. Something crazy. Something reckless that no sane person would ever do. I'm asking you to love me back. Love me as much as I know your boundless heart can. Love me without any more reservation and fear. Love me in spite of me. You know me, all my inadequacies and faults and frustrations. You have seen the man I am time and time again, and I have seen the woman you are. Why are we so quick to doubt each other, to think we would do the other harm when all our heart knows that love is gentle and seeks only to heal?

I think our fault is this: we think that love is too good to be true. That we are unworthy, that we would not recognize it when we see it. We are human, and humanity is feeble. We fear our own faults and think, worst of all, that no one will love us because of the many we possess. We fear the faults of others, especially when we love them. We think there must be some hidden evil lurking under the surface, that the same dark side of our own souls is in the souls of even those we love the most.

But I know your soul. I know it as though in making you God had cleaved a piece of my own soul and pressed it into you. Our hearts are the same, and so are our aims. We both want this love. We want the things we could build together; an incredible career, a family that will be a blessing to the world, a life that is good, peaceful, quiet, and built on a foundation of love. Life is short, and we do not have much time to achieve all these aims, so long as we are apart and living such a cautious, careful life.

I know that you have been burned. I know this choice is hard for you, with fear and anticipation clouding your way. I respect any decision you come to make. But if this is the first decision that shapes the rest of our lives, I want to give my input. It is a simple suggestion: love me. I wouldn't ask such a bold question if I didn't think you had the power and the strength to answer my call with all your passion and power. Love me and be with me. It sounds crazy, to love fearlessly and to build a life together, to build a life of our dreams. It may be crazy of me to even ask such a thing of you. But let's be crazy together. Crazy, fearlessly in love.

My heart is yours forever,

Vikram

Nineteen

Vikram knew he had to do something. And sitting in his house and pondering over a piece of paper was not sufficient.

He glanced at the clock, it was six in the evening. Where had the day gone by? He wondered. Suddenly he recalled the previous day, it was around this hour when Ashok had informed him of his horrid actions. Vikram knew he had to take actions. And determined to make it right, he dialled the number of his worst enemy now.

Vikram asked Ashok to meet him at a bar near the office. Ashok, though mocked Vikram for his unnecessary attempts to bribe him, agreed.

"I will see you in an hour then," Ashok's cheerful voice rang in Vikram's ears. Vikram agreed and hung up.

Vikram bounced on his heels as he waited. Five minutes passed. Ten minutes passed. Then fifteen! Vikram started to worry. What if Ashok didn't show. He decided to give him another fifteen minutes. He waited for almost an hour when Ashok finally turned up. Vikram was too desperate – and had no other option – to meet him.

"Sorry Vikram," Ashok started, though he was not at all sorry. "Unlike you, I have a job, and I have to work!" The snarky comment bothered Vikram, but he just nodded and asked Ashok to sit.

They ordered their drinks, and Vikram started.

"Why?" Vikram asked.

Ashok gave Vikram a shrewd look and then started to laugh. Vikram waited for Ashok to reveal the truth, but he didn't. Vikram tried again, "We are not in office. No one is around here. Please Ashok, for our age-old friendship. Why did you ruin me and why did you do that to Sahana?"

Vikram was pleading and Ashok relished it. It was clear to Vikram that Ashok wanted to break him, and it was clear that he was successful. Ashok swallowed a mouthful of his Scotch, sighed and spoke, "You know why."

"That's it, Ashok, I don't know," Vikram begged mercifully.

"I made a mistake, Vik. Between you and me, as friends, I made a mistake. I thought that if I kissed Sahana, she would be mine, like all your past girlfriends. But she didn't. She accused me of molestation and ran away," Ashok paused to take another long sip. Vikram resisted an urge to hit him. "She ran into your arms Vikram. You have no idea how I felt. Losing a woman, whom I wanted, to you," he snarled, taking yet another sip.

"So, you instead framed me?" Vikram spoke in disbelief, and Ashok just shrugged. "You didn't even consider what would happen to my career? My family? My life? My love?" the last words were barely audible. The look on Ashok's face clearly said that his old friend literally didn't care.

"Why did you spread rumors about Sahana?" Vikram continued.

"So that she starts to hate you, and find solace in me," Ashok took another gulp. He was getting drunk by every sip, and Vikram was finding it easy to get all the relevant details from him.

"How did you know about her virginity status?" Vikram asked after a pause. A pause that was long enough for Ashok to drain two glasses of Scotch.

Ashok gave a sinister laugh while Vikram waited.

"She is a beauty," Ashok hissed, "And when I saw her on top of you, her bare skin shining in the moonlight, I realized what I had missed." Vikram clenched his fists to control his rage. Ashok had just made very rude gestures regarding Sahana's naked body. They offended Vikram to the farthest extent. "Anyways, the way she was fluttering on top of you, I knew it then," Ashok spoke, banging his glass on the table and picking up another drink. Vikram wanted to clarify, ask a million questions, but Ashok continued, "But I knew for sure when I read about it in your journal."

His words came crashing down on Vikram. *Ashok had read his diary?* When? How? Ashok gave a mirthless laugh at his expressions and continued. "Remember when we used to crash at your place sometimes?" Ashok asked, and Vikram nodded, unable to believe his former friend. "I made a copy of your house key." If Vikram's eyes could pop open more, they would have bulged out of his eye sockets at this declaration. Ashok didn't notice his reaction and continued, "I followed you both to your apartment that day. I waited. My heart wrenched at the thought of you having her for the entire night." Vikram winced at the venom in his tone. "I saw you both leave for breakfast. I knew that you must have written the·details of your night with Sahana in your pathetic diary, so I broke in your apartment, and well, you know what happened next."

Vikram's face was contorted with rage, still he composed himself and asked with gritted teeth, "So you Ashok, you read my diary. Read about the most intimate details of our relationship. And spread them in the office under the pretense that I had intentionally shared them with you." Ashok laughed loudly and nodded.

"You are a pathetic bastard," Vikram hissed.

"Not as pathetic as you are though," Ashok was laughing still.

"Yeah?" Vikram was swarming with rage. "We will see about that," and with that, he pulled out his phone from under the table. Pressed the 'stop' button on the audio recorder app and stormed out.

*

Ashok followed him haphazardly. His laughter had vanished, and a worried look replaced it.

"What have you done?" Ashok demanded, trying to snatch his phone.

"Nothing worse than what you have," Vikram hissed as he ran outside, typing in haste. He had to send the recording before Ashok could do anything. Vikram had just pressed 'Send' with a hasty message when something hit his head with brute force.

He staggered a bit and turned around. Ashok had picked up a log from the street and had hit him with all his might. The murderous expressions on Ashok's face scared Vikram. Ashok swung the log again, and this time hit him in the back. Vikram fell on the ground, his phone falling feet away.

Ashok rushed and picked up the phone and checked it. Vikram had sent the audio recording to Sahana and Nalini through WhatsApp with a message, 'Save this recording, quick.'

"Do you know you can delete WhatsApp messages now?" Ashok spoke with a smirk as he sat in front of him. Vikram raised his hand to take back his phone, but Ashok hit him the third time, now with his own phone.

He showed Vikram as he deleted the messages from both girls' chat boxes. And then with a devilish grin, he wiped all his contents. As he pressed 'Format this phone' button, he muttered, "This is to ensure that there are no traces of that recording left on your phone." And with that declaration he threw Vikram's phone back in his face, got up, and walked away. Leaving his long-term best friend all alone on the road!

Twenty

Vikram didn't remember when or how he had come back home. The last thing he recalled was Ashok giving him a sadistic laugh and wiping his phone. Any hope he ever had of clearing his name and getting Sahana back was wiped off with all the contents.

Vikram woke as his phone rang. His whole body was hurting horribly, and it surprised him to realize that he was sleeping with that pain. He didn't know who was calling him as no numbers were now stored in his mobile. He picked it up slowly.

"Vikram," her voice was sweet on the other end of the line, if only because she was speaking his name, "I've got you here on the phone. I'll have you muted and in my pocket, but I'm about to do the maddest thing I've ever done and I... I just didn't want to be alone. I just wanted you to hear me."

"I can hear you," he said into the receiver, but she did not respond, so he tried again. "Sahana, I can hear you. Can you hear--" He wanted to tell her so much, inform her about the last night's incidence, but she was not responding.

"I've got the phone recording, so I'll be able to record anything he says and play it back to Mr. Patil if I need," she said, interrupting him. When she said that, Vikram's blood ran cold. He knew Ashok was not going to fall for the same trick twice. And if he realized what Sahana was doing, he would hurt her.

He knew where she was even as she said, "I'm right outside the door to the sales department. My hands are shaking. How pathetic! I've got to be brave if I'm going to confront him. And I'm going to confront him. I'm already here. There's no turning back now."

"Sahana, wait!" he said, knowing his words were falling on deaf ears, "Please don't confront him alone, he would expect this..." But Sahana was not listening. Vikram heard her tap Ashok's door.

It was dangerous. He'd already hurt Sahana, shoving her against the wall. He'd left marks on her skin with the force of his assault. And that was Ashok at peace, not this wild and cornered Ashok who was willing to ruin Vikram's career and destroy Sahana's life just to save his skin.

But he couldn't make it to the office in time. He wouldn't be able to reach her if Ashok decided to strike out and hurt her. And he couldn't risk getting off the phone with her to call Nalini, who might not answer him anyways. He was trapped on one end of a phone, only able to listen as Sahana marched to war.

He could not make out what it was Ashok said, but he heard Sahana's response, devastating and cutting, her voice clear as glass. Maybe the phone was hiding the tremor in her voice. Maybe her nerves had steeled the second she'd come face to face with the monster they'd once thought of as a friend. "Stand and face me if you think you're a man," she snarled, "I know what you're doing, and you won't get away with it. You may have violated my body, you may have violated my privacy, hiding in the shadows like a creep and watching what was one of the most beautiful moments of my life. You may sully that precious memory, but I won't let you dirty my future. This ends now."

"You have no idea what I'm doing," Ashok said. His voice was quieter than Vikram had expected, but the note of poison in it was all Ashok. Vikram wondered how he had ever missed it. It had been there for so long, it was a wonder he hadn't overdosed on it already. It might have done permanent damage.

"Ruining Vikram's reputation? Trying to protect your own? I don't care about your reasons for your monstrous acts," she spat, all her righteous fury stabbing into Ashok like knives. "Your feelings are none of my concern. I even hope that your heart breaks, and that hideous pit of venom in your stomach destroys you from the inside. The only thing I care about is stopping you."

"Stop me? I'm doing this for you," Ashok insisted, and Vikram heard the muffled thump of Ashok's fist on his desk. "To keep you safe from that loser. You might think your life is ruined, but in five years, when he's no more than a distant memory in your mind, you'll be grateful he was never allowed the opportunity to wreak more havoc in your life than he already has."

"I can't believe you," she snarled, but he cut her off.

"Where is your phone?" he demanded curtly.

"What?" Sahana was shocked by the question, but Vikram expected it. He jumped on his heels helplessly. Why didn't Sahana discuss her plan with him? He would have stopped her.

"Here it is," she spoke. There was a small pause, and then Ashok spoke, "Turn it off and put in on the desk."

Vikram stood confused in his room as he heard Sahana's footsteps. 'What was happening?'

"What do you see in a man like Vikram, anyways?" Ashok continued in a relaxed tone, and Vikram could hear his mockery dripping from his lips, "Is he sweet to you? Such a sensitive shoulder for you to cry on? Some prissy little poet who can charm you with a well-placed word?"

"He's far more than that," Sahana insisted, but Vikram scoffed.

"He's nothing more than that. I've known him longer than you. I've seen the way he lives. His spine is as stiff as that of a book. It cracks under the first sign of pressure. He's a coward. Childish. Lives with his head in the clouds. He'll never have enough money or enough strength to truly be the man a woman like you deserves."

"It's not about what I deserve or don't deserve," Sahana insisted, "life isn't a game in which you measure out your attributes and find the person most suited to your lifestyle. We don't have control over love. But even if we were able to control it, I would have chosen Vikram, with his kindness and his beautiful poetry, over you with your full bank account and an empty heart."

"You're just like every other girl," Ashok laughed, dry. From the other end of the line Vikram took in every word that was said with quiet fury, unable to protest anything he was hearing but glad it would be recorded so that someone would believe that this was the core of Ashok's rotten heart. "Everyone who has ever been with him. At first, he charms them, but then they find that all his substance is in creativity, sensitivity. He'd rather bring you a book than flowers. He'd rather write a poem than hold your hand. He has no confidence. He has no power. He's nothing like me."

"And thank God for that!" Sahana exclaimed, and the relief in her voice was palpable. Vikram worried Ashok might think she was mocking him. "I could never love a man like you. Vikram is a good man with a pure soul and love in his heart that you will never understand."

"I understand love," Ashok said darkly, his voice an animal growl. "I'm in love with you."

Vikram couldn't believe it. He'd never heard such a farce made of the term. The idea that Ashok's violence and hideousness could be misconstrued by anyone, even himself, as something akin to love seemed laughable. But it was impossible for Vikram to laugh while Sahana was in such imminent danger.

"That doesn't matter," Sahana replied, her voice as cool as stream water, "I will never love you back. So, learn to move on with your life and stop ruining mine with your lies and your rumors, as hideous as your soul."

"I won't move on," Ashok insisted, "I want you."

"Take a step back," Sahana countered, and Vikram could hear the barest hint of fear creeping into her throat. Again, he tried to calculate how long it would take him to be there. If there was someone he could call for help. He remembered his laptop and fired off a quick email to Nalini.

I know you don't trust me, but Sahana is unsafe. In Ashok's office, he is enraged. All will be revealed, but it doesn't matter now. Call security. HELP HER. -V

"I'll stay where I am," Ashok said, nearly purring, "but I want you. I want you to come to me. You think I don't care for you. That I'm a sick, selfish man, and that may be so. But you don't need this job, not really. You don't need the reputation of dating Vikram Shan of all people, that worthless sensitive fool. All will be well when you're on my arm instead, I'll make sure of it. And when you're in my bed-- I'll blow your mind. You'll starve for my touch. You'll never want to leave my bed. You'll call me at all hours begging for it. Your first time was with Vikram. You don't know what good love-making feels like."

"Repulsive," Sahana whispered, and Vikram couldn't help but agree. His stomach was roiling with fear.

Vikram wanted to yell, beg her to get out, but didn't dare. What if Ashok heard his voice and hurt Sahana?

Ashok wasn't finished, though. If Sahana were safe behind a wall of glass, Vikram would have been gleeful at the words coming from his former friend's mouth. With every hideous thing he said, he was digging his own grave deeper and deeper. Vikram could only hope the recording on Sahana's phone was picking up as much of what Ashok was saying as Vikram could hear. But Sahana wasn't safe yet. Vikram couldn't rest easy.

"You just don't understand," Ashok said, "playing at a career, like a child trying on her father's suits. It's stupid. And you're not a stupid woman. I think you know deep down, a woman's place is serving a good man, the kind of man who can provide everything she needs. I'm that man. I'm the man for you. It doesn't matter if you love me. You're a practical girl. I'm your best option."

Sahana laughed then, bright as the sun, "I have a good man, who is kind and honest and whose pockets are never empty, who laughs with me and loves me and has already enriched my life with more happiness than all the money in the world could bring."

Ashok snorted. "If you think the person of the most worth to you in this whole world is Vikram Shan, you've never experienced true wealth a day in your life. Come with me. Just out to dinner. I could show you more opulence than you've ever known. Something that a woman like you should have had at hand all her life. You'll forget all about the pitying sympathy you've mistaken for love and feel what true love is."

"The only thing I feel for you is pity," Sahana said softly, and he could hear her heading back towards the office door. Vikram could only pray that Ashok wouldn't stop her when she tried to leave. "You're so twisted, Ashok. You're so far from anything that love actually is. You may know the value of a Rolex watch or a Maserati, but you see no value in the gentle fall of rain, the blooming of a jasmine flower, coffee with a friend, the glow of the moon. You've never read something that's made your heart sing or bared your soul to an empty page. You've never been vulnerable, so you cannot understand strength. And you've never loved, so you could not understand me if I tried to love you. You're sick, but it is not my job to make you well."

"You'll think about my offer," Ashok said, his voice muted a little with the distance between them. Vikram felt his breathing come easier. "Maybe not at your desk, where everyone can see. Maybe in your room late at night when no one's watching, and it's just you and me within your thoughts. You'll think about being mine. You'll find that you like the idea."

"I'd rather fling myself off a bridge than run into your arms," Sahana snarled. Vikram heard the creak of the door opening, "but thank you," Sahana added, "for being so forthcoming, and for speaking loudly and clearly enough to be heard on this recording. When I present it to Mr. Patil this afternoon, he'll surely be swayed by your strong argument as to why you should be fired and never allowed back into an office setting."

"You crazy bitch!" Ashok roared, and then Vikram truly felt fear like he never had before. He could have teleported to her, reached out his arms across the city just so save her. If only magic were real. Because he heard sounds that wouldn't have made it onto the recording of a civilized conversation. The shattering of glass, a whimper of fear from Sahana, a cut off plea. The smack of a fist against flesh.

"Sahana!" Vikram screamed, "Sahana!"

But, of course, she couldn't hear him. He could do nothing for her. It was only in the next flurry of activity that he heard the voice of the company security guard, Nihan, whom before today Vikram had only ever heard in conversation. Now he was shouting, "Back away, back away from her!"

"That crazy whore! That evil woman! She and her pathetic lover are conspiring against me!" Ashok shrieked. He sounded crazy. "She hit me! She's blacked my eye!"

Then Sahana's voice, tremoring with fear but still managing to sound clear and strong as the dawn, "I'd like to report Ashok for sexual as well as verbal and physical harassment. He has created a work environment that is beyond hostile and run a smear campaign to wreck my reputation."

"Your reputation?" Ashok laughed, "it's my reputation she and Vikram are out to ruin. I was only defending myself when she threw herself at me, hoping to seduce me into saving her skin."

"Right, of course," Nihan drawled. It was obvious that he did not believe Ashok. "And the phone call I got from Nalini in marketing reporting that Sahana's life was in danger?"

"It's doctored! It's a conspiracy!" Ashok shouted, loud enough to make Vikram recoil from the speaker.

"It's all on the voice recording," Sahana assured the security guard, "it'll have everything Mr. Patil needs to know."

"She is lying," Ashok snarled. "Her phone is lying on my desk." And Vikram heard Ashok scuttle to his desk.

"What you don't know," Sahana spoke, her voice suddenly growing loud. Vikram assumed that she was pulling out the phone from her pocket, "that I carry two phones," Vikram heard a smirk in Sahana's voice. Vikram was proud of her, such a brilliant plan. Ashok, believing he was not being recorded, spoke what truly was on his mind. His true intentions.

"You'll report before Mr. Patil for a disciplinary hearing tomorrow morning," Nihan told Ashok, "but for now, I'll have to escort you from the premises. This is disappointing, Ashok," he added, "I'd always thought you were an okay guy."

"I'll clear my name," Ashok threatened, "I'll make Mr. Patil see reason. He'll understand that this crazy woman--"

"Goodbye, Ashok," Sahana said, "I hope we never meet again."

With that, the noise in the background quieted, and it was just Vikram and Sahana on the line.

"Vikram," she said, "I'm safe now. Did you hear what happened?"

"Yeah," he breathed, too amazed to say much more. His heart was pounding in his chest. Nalini had believed him. He'd managed to save Sahana after all. "I heard every word."

Twenty-One

Tears of joy and relief streaked down Vikram's face as he washed his last dish and set it in the drying rack. He'd nearly bleached his apartment clean, unsure of what else to do with his hands until they were holding Sahana once more. He'd felt a tremble in them since he put down the phone. He'd caught up on all the work he could do from home and the thought of beginning to put pen to paper when it came to processing what he was feeling seemed, for once, too overwhelming. He called his mother and told her all that had happened. He hadn't spoken to her since he'd met Sahana, too scared of disappointing her with another relationship that couldn't be. But this was love. This was true. And it hurt. His parents had been married for more than thirty years. If anyone knew about a love that stood the test of time, it was them.

"My son," his mother said, and he could hear her searching for words over the line. "Even this sorrow is good.

From this egg of sadness, a bird of joy will burst forth, and sing a song like you have never heard. This misunderstanding has allowed you to listen closely to the pattern of each other's hearts. Pray she finds you worthy and true. And clean your room. The love of your life will be there soon."

So, he'd scrubbed the countertops and even dusted the fan blades in a blind search for something to do. Vikram had never been the one for spring cleaning. But he wanted his home to be a haven for Sahana, a place where she could rest after the horror she'd gone through today.

Vikram ran a dishcloth over the countertops in his bathroom, catching a glimpse of his strange face in the mirror. Tear-streaked but brimming with happiness, a jaw so sore from smiling that he wished he could stop. How strange his life had been since he first met Sahana. He was tired of the story. He was looking forward to their happily ever after.

And that happily ever after should start with clean sheets, he thought, stripping his bed down and leaving his dirty bedding in the laundry hamper. The fresh sheets he pulled across his mattress were white, bare, nothing to write home about.

But with Sahana, he could see potential-- silk and soft, fresh laundered and smelling of Jasmine and soap. He could see the walls painted a pale blue, nothing fancy, just enough to really let the light from the sun streaming through the windows bathe everything in a pure morning glow. He could see a bedspread she'd picked, bookshelves spilling over with both their books, her dresses hanging in the closet next to his pressed shirts. He could see the hallway, now bare, instead hanging with pictures of beloved family and friends. He could see his ratty old couch replaced with something new and plush and comfortable where they could hold each other on rainy days and read long into the night, her head on his chest, flipping the pages in tandem. Every time his mind strayed to Sahana, a new life bloomed in front of his eyes. If only she were there with him now.

The sun was setting and she still had not returned. Maybe she had gone home to her apartment, too overwhelmed to even think about running into his arms tonight. He'd understand, even without a phone call, if she crawled into her own bed instead of his, lying there in the dark and dreaming alone. After the day she'd been through, he'd understand anything she did was what she needed to do. Still, he made enough *chana dal* for two, his mother's recipe that she'd picked up from a friend in New Delhi, the one he'd learned just in case he ever had someone he needed to impress. Impressing Sahana was high stakes indeed. He wanted to impress her into staying for the rest of her life. So, he simmered the split chickpeas in stock and spices, set the rice to cook, and checked his watch as the whole meal came together. Sahana was from New Delhi originally. He wondered if this was a meal she'd eaten often as a child, one she thought of with love in her heart. He hoped so. He hoped he could offer some comfort. That she'd come to think of him as home.

Finally, there was a knock on the door. Vikram sprang into action, tea towel still draped over his shoulder, making a mental note to uncork the bottle of white wine he'd left chilling in the fridge. Sahana would probably want a drink after all the hell she'd been through. He wouldn't blame her.

But he never wanted to taste scotch again. It held too many bitter memories in its depths.

He opened his door, and all the breath went out of his lungs. He shut it again, hard, reaching into his pocket for his phone. His phone-- that was still on the kitchen table. Ashok was at the door.

He knocked again. "Vikram," he called through the closed door. "I know I've done wrong. I know I don't have any right to ask. But will you please let me in? There's no one else I can turn to. I've burned every bridge I have."

Vikram could have laughed. The first bridge Ashok had torched was Vikram. "Burning down the world to pick yourself out of the ashes wasn't the best plan you could have had," he told Ashok. "Go home before I call the police."

"You have every right to be angry," Ashok said. "What I did was unforgivable."

"Then leave knowing I don't forgive you. I hope I never see you again." Vikram was not this person. He didn't hold resentment in his heart like this. He wasn't bitter and hateful. What had Ashok turned him into?

"Your supper smells good from this side of the door," Ashok said, "I never thought to learn how to cook. Knew I'd never be a family man. Take out and street food all my life."

Vikram didn't say anything. He placed his ear against the door. He could hear Ashok shifting, settling down with his back to Vikram's door. He was probably drunk again. When wasn't he drunk? Vikram saw more red flags now as he looked back at Ashok's last year. Maybe there was something he could have said, something he could have done to save Ashok. But now there was nothing redeemable.

"The thing about you, Vikram, that I don't get is this: how one man, objectively average. Not that smart. Not that handsome. No real shine to you. Quiet in public. How one average man with a dead-end job and a dead-end life could spend so much time hoping, dreaming about the future. Didn't you know you were wrong to dream? Didn't someone tell you?" Vikram was tempted to open the door just to hit Ashok in the back of the head. "I tried to protect you. Tried to align your expectations with what you should truly have. But you were always the dreamer, and I couldn't change that about you."

There was a muffled sob through the door. "And in trying to change you, I made a mistake. I fell in love. I ruined my own life, and now she hates me and wants you. Congratulations, Vikram, you get my job, the woman of my dreams, the life I built, all handed to you."

Vikram could care less about Ashok's crocodile tears. His attention had caught on something Ashok had said. Something he didn't like. Ashok said that Vikram had his job. It had always been rumored that if there ever were an internal promotion in sales, Vikram would take over the office Ashok had kept for so many years. Vikram had always thought it was a ridiculous pipe dream. Ashok had always handled his job well, enjoyed it, even. He was shiny and golden, but now that his reputation had been tarnished, someone else would need to step up to the plate. Someone who could. Quiet Vikram had never dreamed of being the scotch and cigars type of man's man needed to make sales happen. Would he really be promoted in a situation like this?

Ashok scoffed as though Vikram had asked, "Oh, Mr. Patil hasn't said anything yet. At least not to me. He stared at me with that sick look of disappointment in his eyes and slid a pre-written resignation letter over his desk at me. Pre-written. It was a form letter. An over and done with sort of thing, after so many years of work." he sighed again, and Vikram heard a thump that must have been Ashok slamming his forehead against the wood of Vikram's door, "I knew it was over. Even before he called me into his office. No doubt you're the next one on his short-list. You've always known it was a possibility. I bet you're boiling over with glee."

At that, Vikram could stand it no longer. The irritating feeling like a mosquito buzzing a hairs-breadth from his skin made contact and blossomed into red rage. He opened his door, nearly knocking over the miserable lump of man on his doorstep in the process. Ashok looked up at him, bleary and a little drunk. His suit was wrinkled and his eyes were red-rimmed. At another point, Vikram might have felt sympathy. Now all he felt was disgust. "I feel absolutely no glee to see you fall like this. I'm not *you,* for God's sake. I don't enjoy the suffering of others. It's not something I attempted to cause you."

Ashok blustered, "*Lies!* You and Sahana orchestrated--"

"*You* orchestrated your own downfall, Ashok," Vikram snarled. "How quick you are to blame others for your failures. Your meddling, your jealousy, your insane rage, it all piled on top of you until it crushed you underneath it. And some part of you always knew it would. I don't think you're shocked right now. I think you're disappointed that you weren't able to dig yourself out of a hole. But that's the thing about meddling-- it'll never lift you towards the moral high ground. It just brings you closer and closer to hell."

"Such a *poet*, Vikram. Such sentiment. How *pretty*," was Ashok's sardonic reply, but Vikram cut him off.

"You're just a fool, Ashok. You've always thought that to be a man was to cut yourself off from any feelings but rage and pride. You've always thought that to read, to cook, to take any time devoted to the sweetness of this life, was to be womanly. And you've always hated women worst of all, thinking of them as little more than conquests, things that you could fuck and discard. It's repulsive."

"None of your girlfriends seemed to mind it," Ashok hissed, but Vikram laughed. He was so far above the dull barbs Ashok could still craft. They could not strike him.

"You wonder why you have no love in your life? You've never wanted it. You thought you could live apart from it, and you have. These are the fruits of your beliefs. Bitter as they are. They're the meal you've ordered. Now eat it. Get off my doorstep and out of my life."

Ashok rolled his eyes, a grin on his face that might have been sad if there weren't so much madness within it, "If I leave now, you'll never truly be rid of me. Even if Sahana chooses you and I never see her again, I'll still be there in the middle of your relationship You may think of me as a stain, cancer, I don't care. I'm a wedge between you both. You'll never fit right together. There will always be tension. There will always be friction. There will always be me."

"Is that the best you can aspire to be at this point in your bold and glorious life?" Vikram asked, his arms crossed across his chest, "is it your wildest dream to be an antagonist in someone else's love story? You wanted Sahana, and you couldn't have her--"

"THAT'S THE PROBLEM!" Ashok shouted, struggling unsteadily to his feet. "I always get what I want. I want her. I want her…"

Vikram pressed his hand against Ashok's chest to keep him from stumbling into the apartment. It was a careful balance, to keep the drunk man from falling down the stairwell but also keep him from coming inside. "You don't want her. You just want someone else's toys, like a child on a playground, but Sahana is her own person. She's not a toy. Whether or not she loves me, she'll never love you as long as you treat her like an object. That much is certain."

"I want something of my own, earned on my own merit, not just with my charms. Trying to keep her away from you was fun at first, but as she denied me and denied me, it became infuriating. I couldn't stand losing the way I was. None of my old tricks worked." Ashok slumped, a defeated man. He reeked of alcohol. How strange to watch someone so lauded fall apart in the blink of an eye. Someone who had once worn a pressed suit, who was now more wrinkles than he was straight lines. Vikram couldn't help it. He felt pity, even though he knew all Ashok's problems were his own fault. "I'd hoped in pursuing her I could become a better person," Ashok muttered into his hands.

Vikram knelt, lifting his old friend's chin to meet his gaze. "Instead, you became a monster. But your life isn't over. There's still breath in your lungs. You can rebuild from here. Maybe in a different city. Maybe in a different country. And maybe you'll never build back what you once were. But that's the beauty of breathing. You can always start again."

Ashok gave a watery smile, and for a moment they were college students again, young with every possibility unfurling before them. "You're a good friend," Ashok said to him. "I'm sorry I lost you."

"Me too," Vikram agreed and was surprised to find out that he meant it. "Goodnight, Ashok." And he watched his old friend disappearing into the darkness, walking away for the last time.

Twenty-Two

Vikram woke to his phone ringing. The company phone number flashed across the screen. He answered it. "Please wait for Mr. Patil," the secretary's voice said on the other line. Then there was a ringing noise and Mr. Patil spoke.

"Vikram," he greeted. His tone was hard to puzzle out. Vikram prided himself as someone who understood others, but Mr. Patil had always been an inscrutable mystery to him. He couldn't tell if the man was about to fire or promote him. This was the moment. This was what his life had been building towards since meeting Sahana. So many things had been set in motion. Now all that was left to do was live through them.

"Mr. Patil," Vikram replied. There was silence over the line. Vikram struggled for something to say. "Are you well?" he finished lamely.

"I have had better weeks," the other man said. Again, Vikram couldn't decide if he was disappointed or amused. Maybe neither. Maybe he was just resigned to Vikram's fate and ready to get on with the company he was running. Maybe he'd decided Vikram was an acceptable loss – he had to be if Mr. Patil had given up Ashok, his golden boy, so easily. Mr. Patil was a shrewd businessman. In the end, his fondness for any particular employee did not matter. His fondness for his company's wellness came first. He would do whatever it took to make sure the company survived, and if that meant carving Vikram and the rest of Ashok's poisoned sales department away like a cancer and rehiring each position, Vikram did not think Mr. Patil would hesitate.

"Sir--" he started to say, but Mr. Patil cut him off.

"When is the soonest you can come in?"

"I can be in a taxi cab in five minutes," Vikram said. "Will that suit?"

"I'll be waiting. See you soon." The line went dead. Vikram stared at the black screen of his phone, wondering what would happen to him. There was nothing else he could do. He had to meet his fate.

When he arrived in the lobby of M.R. Enterprises, as clinically clean as ever with its stainless steel and polished glass door, its wide-open windows letting in the noon light and its primly dressed receptionist, he felt out of place, as though he'd been run over and nearly drowned before finding himself dripping all his sorrow and fear onto the waxed floors. He caught the curious glances of his coworkers-- it was hard not to meet their gazes. Everyone was looking at him. But he'd done nothing to feel the shame burning in his cheeks with the force of their gazes. How unfortunate to be a spectacle when all he wanted was to be an observer, to create scenes in his notebook rather than living them out before the eyes of others. That was the life of a writer, the dream he held. He hadn't wanted to live out anything worth writing about.

He swiped his card without meeting anyone's gaze, moving as fast as he could away from the whole office's line of sight. He felt their gazes on the back of his neck, ducking his head to avoid the sensation as much as he could. He heard whispering and didn't bother trying to distinguish what they were saying. Did they know he'd been wronged, or would he always be the villain in their eyes? In that moment, he hated Ashok worse than ever.

Vikram took the stairs, two by two, already halfway to his desk at the sales department through sheer force of muscle memory before realizing he needed to take the elevator to the top floor. There was a woman waiting by the elevator. Vikram did a double-take, his mind on Sahana, but it was not Sahana. It was his dear friend, Nalini, looking tired with a mug of coffee still in hand.

His blood ran cold. For the first time since Sahana hung up the phone, true fear rushed through him. He wanted Mr. Patil's respect and hoped for his job back, but he hadn't realized, until he lost it, how much he needed Nalini's friendship. Especially after losing Ashok in such a horrible way, the thought of losing Nalini too was too much to bear. Nalini had always been true and careful with him. She'd been so happy to see him get together with Sahana. He feared she'd never trust him again -- not after what the whole office thought he did.

But as he approached her, her face shone, first shocked and then elated. She held up a finger, asking him to wait, and set her coffee mug directly onto the floor. "Vikram!" She squealed, throwing her arms around his neck in an affectionate hug.

"Thanks for not pouring coffee on me," Vikram said into her shoulder, breathing in the comforting scent of her perfume. "Have you seen Sahana?"

Nalini pulled away and mimed smacking his shoulder. "Ideally I'd be angry that you're hugging me while thinking of another woman, but under the circumstances, I know why you'd be so concerned. I have seen her. She's in her office. That poor woman."

"Is she okay?" He asked her. She shook her head.

"Would you be? I've been wearing myself into a splinter trying to defend her from the hideousness of this office. First, I thought you were the enemy. Then I heard your voice message and then that email you sent-- they said security dragged Ashok from his office. What a monster. And I never knew!" Nalini looked on the verge of tears.

"None of us knew," he assured her. "Hey wait! You heard my voice message?" Vikram asked, shocked.

"It was you who sent it, isn't it?" Nalini asked skeptically.

"Yes, but Ashok had forced the phone out of my hands, and had deleted the WhatsApp message,"

"Oh, that's why the message was deleted the next minute. Luckily, I was sitting on my laptop and chatting via web-WhatsApp. I saw your message and downloaded it instantly. But I didn't hear it instantly. I was so mad at you that I heard it only when I reached home yesterday after work!" Nalini admitted with a guilty look.

"I don't blame you. I would have called you or Sahana to tell everything, but the bastard had even wiped my phone. I could not even call for help!" Vikram spoke exasperatedly.

"Help?" Nalini asked wide-eyed. And Vikram narrated how Ashok had attacked him. Nalini's mouth fell open at this.

"If I'd known what a monster he was, I keep thinking I could have stopped him. But there's no going back. I don't know what will happen now."

Nalini grabbed his wrist, her expression more intense than he'd ever seen it. "I wouldn't say there's no way to save you. There's a lot of people in this office who are your friends. Who are Sahana's friends. Who are friends of the two of you, together. The best thing about the spectacle Ashok made out of leaving is that everyone knows something went wrong-- something that he did. Gossip moves quickly. The truth will out itself soon enough. And when it does, it will take some time to rebuild your happiness. And know that we'll be behind you."

Vikram sighed. His heart hurt.

"And…" Nalini said with an expression that he could not read, "here," and she handed him a flash drive. "It contains your conversation with Ashok where he admitted everything. I gave a copy of it to Sahana this morning, she must have heard it by now. But I haven't shared it with anyone else. It was very personal, I am honored to realize that you trust me enough," Nalini finished with a smile and a warm hug.

Mr. Patil was waiting for him at the top of the elevator, and Sahana was somewhere in the office building, brave enough to show her face even after all the slander and abuse she'd faced at the hands of Ashok. He had to be brave too. Even after the stares he'd gotten. Sahana had gotten so much worse. "I don't know what will happen to me, Nalini," he said. "If Mr. Patil fired Ashok--"

Nalini gripped his shoulder, giving it a firm shake. "That's not going to happen to you. Ashok was fired for doing something wrong. We all know now that you did nothing wrong. You fell in love. You tried to remain dutiful and honorable, and that viper in the grass struck when no one expected it. You're involved, sure, but you're not to blame."

"I just don't know," he sighed.

"I do. I know that in the end, love will save you. It saves us all." Nalini released his shoulder. "Now face Mr. Patil and know that we're all behind you."

Vikram nodded and stepped dizzily onto the elevator, his head spinning. He was so emboldened by her words that when he walked into Mr. Patil's office, he didn't even shake the man's hand before saying, "Mr. Patil, I just want to be happy. Sahana and I, we were in love, are in love, I hope, and Ashok tried to ruin us. I know it was messy and potentially ruinous, but I truly believe that we can live through this. With your blessing and consent, I'd like to return to work as soon as possible. I'd like to see that no further harm comes to Sahana and that new programs are implemented to fight the kind of harassment that occurred at Ashok's hand."

Mr. Patil blinked once. Then a smile spread across his face. "Well, hello to you, too, Vikram. I like what you have to say. Let's talk."

Vikram explained, from the start, what had happened between him and Ashok. The patterns of behavior that had once seemed harmless and then convalesced into a nightmare in which Sahana's life was nearly destroyed. Ashok's confession recorded in a flash drive. Seeing Ashok on his doorstep, the conversations they'd had, and threats that were exchanged. For the sake of clarity, he left nothing out. Winded from his conversation, he finally paused.

Mr. Patil was quiet for a long moment, fingers templed as he took in the information laid out before him. It was something that Vikram had always appreciated about Mr. Patil: he listened closely and didn't speak until he knew exactly what he was going to say. "A lot of this information I knew already, of course, but I was blind to so much. When you only evaluate professionally, trying to remain as objective as possible to someone's... distasteful personality quirks, as I thought of Ashok's cocksureness before, you can miss an opportunity to evaluate character. That isn't all on me, but I do feel, in part, to blame for what happened here. This harassment went on under my nose, poisoning the atmosphere of my company in a way that it will take months if not years to fully heal from. We will heal, of course, I have no doubt. But faith has been shaken. And people have been hurt. Sahana more than anyone. Tell me, what do you think of her, in the face of all this?"

Vikram didn't hesitate to answer. "I'm in love with her, sir. I always will be. I want what's best for her. Whether she transfers offices or remain here, I'll stand by her decision. I don't care if her future plans factor me into them or if she decides to leave me for good. So long as she's happy, I'll be happy."

At that, Mr. Patil laughed. It was the warmest laugh Vikram had ever heard from his boss, imbibed with true emotion. "Do you know Vikram what Sahana said to me?"

Vikram shook his head. He couldn't imagine.

"She said she only wanted your happiness. That so long as you were still employed, she would leave if she had to. So long as your name was cleared, she'd be content."

With those words, Vikram's heart soared. There was hope for him and Sahana, after all. He hadn't been wrong to dream.

"It would be appropriate now if you go to her. I will not stop you. Let your union be the first steps towards healing the wound that Ashok has wrought across the face of this company. I'll have our human resources officers to handle the rest, they can fix work, but they can't fix a broken relationship."

"Yes sir," Vikram said, "thank you sir."

Vikram remembered a line of poetry, something old and Western from the works of Shakespeare: *"With love's light wings did I o'erperch these walls, For stony limits cannot hold love out, And what love can do, that dares love attempt."* What strange words, spoken by a doomed young man hundreds of years ago, to a woman who would ultimately be his downfall. And yet, before his death, what a love story Romeo lived!

Vikram could feel love's light wings now, guiding him forward to the office where Sahana worked. He wasn't sure what he would do when he got to her. He wasn't sure what he could say, what she wanted to hear. But Vikram trusted the love leading them forward. He knew, beyond a shadow of a doubt, that they would be together and work out all these flaws keeping them apart. There was no other acceptable ending.

Nalini was at her desk when he arrived, and she waved him into Sahana's office with a grin too big to hide inside her coffee cup. Sahana was on the phone, talking with a printing company about a mock-up of some promotional materials. At first, she didn't see Vikram. It gave him a moment to truly take her in, like a bride on her wedding day, evaluating the life they were making together. It would be a good one, he thought, watching her eyes narrow as she argued precise margins and laid out her expectations to the company. She was smart and shrewd, but sweeter than honey and so full of love. It felt like an electric shock every time their hands touched. She was his soulmate, if there was such a thing. He'd always doubted it before meeting her, but now, looking at her, it was like all the books said: he knew.

She caught his eye, and her face dropped its guarded, customer-service look in favor of something softer, more vulnerable. "I'll have to call you back," she said into the phone, "Yes, after lunch will work. Goodbye."

Then she hung up the receiver, and it was the only two of them, standing in silence. She stood up from behind her desk and walked towards him.

"I wanted to say--" he started, but she pressed a finger to his lips.

"I know every word inside your heart. There's no need to speak them. I know who you are."

That was everything Vikram had ever wanted to hear. All his lonely life he'd prayed for an understanding angel, and here she was before him with a finger to his lips. He wished she'd replace it with her own lips.

"Look around," she whispered, "your words are all I see. They're all I hear." And with that, Vikram realized what he was seeing: wallpapering Sahana's desk area was a collage of printed words. All of them were familiar to him. They should have been. After all, each one he'd written by his own hand. His poetry, wrapping her in a cocoon of loving words.

"I love you, and you love me." Sahana said, "every time you kiss me, I taste the poetry in your lips."

"Then let me kiss you again," Vikram whispered, the knowledge that she wanted him thrilling through him as he leaned in to capture her lips. Her head tilted and her smile, like the dawn, blossomed before him, glowing warm as the sun. All the light within her, visible only to Vikram when he closed his eyes, crashed into him like a wave. These kisses, he thought, hands running through her hair, were incredible. Enough to last him the rest of his life.

Twenty-Three

"**Y**ou really cleaned up in here," Sahana remarked as she stood in the doorway. Vikram tried to catch up with his thoughts and not let them overrun him. But here she was in his doorway, ready to walk through his door. Vikram's heart fluttered in his chest, shocking him a little with its insistence on being noticed. He didn't want to pay attention to his heart. He wanted to watch Sahana walk.

"After you," he said, reveling in the minute swivel of her hips as she entered his home. Here she was, back where she belonged, and he could see his future stretched out in front of him as clearly as he could see the pattern of her curls or her mischievous grin, leveled at him over her shoulder as she stood in his kitchen.

"It even looks like you scrubbed the walls. Move-in ready." She blushed as though he realized what she'd just insinuated. He let it slide though, stepping in to kiss her instead. She seemed grateful for the momentary distraction kissing provided, running an exploratory hand over the muscle underneath his t-shirt sleeve, the hem that she was considering pulling over his head. He put a hand on her shoulder and pushed her gently, not to stop her, but to pause.

"I cleaned," he confessed, trying to stop the burble of his thoughts up to his mouth whenever he looked at her. He had no choice but to be true to her. She made him want to spill his guts just so she could approve of their contents. He wanted her to love his every feeling, to approve of all his reasons. "There was nothing else I could do while I was waiting for you. I was so sick and scared, thinking of what might be happening to you. And then Ashok showed up here--"

"He what?" Her voice was measurably colder, her eyes darting around the place as though Ashok might still be in the shadows, waiting to pop out and grab her. Vikram didn't blame her. He remembered the disgust and disturbance he'd felt looking down at his old friend. He'd worried for a moment that Ashok had seen Sahana on his way to Vikram's place.

Vikram shook his head, clearing the leftover cobwebs of fear from his mind. Ashok was gone. They could start the rest of their lives. "It wasn't like that. He was a little drunk, a little belligerent, yes. But he was mostly just pathetic. A man who'd lost everything."

"A man who cost himself everything, you mean," she corrected.

"You're right," he sighed, "I just regret what could have been, had he not decided to go down that road. A friendship

I once valued, even though now I see how rotten it truly was. It's hard to lose something like that."

"Even with all you gained?" Sahana asked, scratching at his scalp with her nails. It felt sensational. Vikram closed his eyes a little, relishing in the contact.

"Even with all I gained," he said.

"That's fair," she told him seriously, "I understand. I know there's a lot that happened that was wrong and painful, even before we got together. And most of that was Ashok's meddling, but some of it was you. And some of it was me."

Vikram sighed, sitting down on the couch. She sat next to him; the line of her thigh pressed against his, hot as fire. He wanted to kiss her again, to sink into her until they were one, and the ghost of this nightmare was fully behind them where it would remain consigned to the past. But for it to truly ever be the past, they needed to talk. "Inability to trust each other. That's been our problem from the start. It's kept us from being fair to each other."

"And fair to ourselves," she added, "I held you at arms' length when I needed you close. And you blamed me when I needed you to see me. We hurt each other, and maybe the traps Ashok planted there for us made it worse, but there's no denying that we did cause each other pain." There was pain in her eyes as she said it, but Vikram had had enough. They had earned a happily ever after. They shouldn't have to hurt any longer.

"We're only human," he told her, "we fail each other from time to time. I can't promise you a life free from pain, even a life free from the pain that I will cause. I know that someday, probably sooner rather than later, I will hurt you or you will hurt me. I hope we forgive each other for it. But we'll do things that are unfair. It would be foolish to promise anything else. Because love isn't about being fair, it's about being human, tender, passionate, raw. Living like that, how can we not hurt and be hurt? We just have to love each other through it. Because the love we feel for each other if we stay open rather than walling ourselves out will be worth it."

Sahana smiled at that, and when she didn't say anything in response Vikram took the initiative to kiss her, once, hard, with all spontaneity and joy. There would be pain. But kisses like this would get them through it. Of that he was certain. He leaned over her as he pressed one hand against her waist and tangled the other in her hair and took another kiss, just because he could, hearing her sigh happily into his mouth as she deepened the kiss. They lay there on the couch, suddenly slow in their movements, her fingers stroking his spine as though he were a beloved book, his lips ghosting across her neck, relishing in the delicious shiver she gave. They were in no hurry. They'd get where they wanted to eventually, but for now, it was hands and mouths, bodies pressed against each other, hotter and heavier by the minute.

"Are we doing this?" she whispered in his ear.

"I... we don't have to do anything you don't--" he started, but she cut him off with another kiss, fingernails scraping down his neck, deliciously dirty and purposeful, heavy with intent.

"Oh, we really have to. I insist," she told him, before scraping her teeth along his neck in a way that made his hold on her hip painfully hard. She seemed to like it, surging up to meet him with more kisses. He pulled her hair out of its ponytail and watched it spill like a waterfall down the arm of his couch, so raven-dark that it was nearly blue. Her eyes were dark with lust, slightly out of focus as she smiled dizzily at him and craned her neck up for another kiss.

He was torn between wanting to do everything and not knowing what to do. What Sahana had done-- but then again, he supposed he knew everything she'd done. She'd only ever been with him. With the world at his fingertips, the door to everything, the one he'd opened for her, he wasn't sure where he wanted to take her.

He wanted to take her as far as she'd possibly let him.

"I know you haven't--" he gasped as her hands found their way under his shirt, "--had a lot of experience, and I don't want to hurt you, or make you think there's anything you have to do... but..."

"I may not have had a lot of physical experience," she told him, "But Vikram, if your memory serves correctly, I'm pretty amazing. I have a mind, and I read a lot of really, really good books. I've got a great imagination and have been waiting for the right guy to make all those dreams a reality. Lucky you," Sahana pressed a kiss to the base of his neck.

"Lucky me," he echoed as she pulled his t-shirt over his head. He said it like he was joking, trying to hide with humor just how much he meant it. Lying there on his couch with her underneath him, her arms around his neck and her lips brushing his throat, he couldn't imagine how fate had led him to this point. All the sorrow they'd had to go through to get to this moment felt unreal in the face of their bodies melding together once more. As she reached up to press her lips to his chin, his throat, his collar bone, almost worshipfully, he lost himself in the rainfall of kisses.

I'm home, I'm home, he thought each time her lips grazed over his skin. As he slipped her shirt off and felt her bare skin touching his, that spark of electricity flowing between them intensified. As his eyes locked onto hers and she nodded, leading him farther-- it felt better than the first time. He wondered if this would ever grow old, if they'd ever get bored of each other when there was no skin left to explore and nothing left to learn. But then he thought of Sahana, smart and powerful and bright, and realized there would always be more to learn. She was complex and beautiful, the sort of puzzle a person could spend their whole lives figuring out. She was the sort of person he could see himself loving for the rest of his life.

Vikram was ready for the rest of his life.

And his life started anew when she took his hand in hers, leading him towards his bedroom without having to pause, as though she'd known the way her whole life. As she lay her head down on his pillow, all her dark hair spilling across his white sheets, she looked up at him with her dark eyes, and he lost himself in their depths, dropping down onto his elbows to pepper kisses across her neck and chest. The warm, soft skin of her stomach felt sweet under his touch, and the whimper she gave each time he pressed his lips there drove him wild. He kissed along the waistband of her pants, and she pushed them away with her thumbs until there was nothing but skin, and skin, and skin. Vikram kept kissing, feeling her nails scraping against his scalp, her fingers tangling in his hair as she pulled a little, urging him upwards, back towards her mouth.

He felt a spark of pleasure as he caught her lip between his teeth, and she groaned, fingers pausing momentarily in their quest to undo his trouser button and cast his belt off. They'd been so patient at first, so deliberate and slow, apt students eager to learn each other's bodies. Fully engaged in the art of memorization. They knew they had the time to take everything they wanted, but this thing between them was so new that they could take a long, luxurious route towards discovering what it truly was that they wanted.

It was easier to wait now that they had moved past the first, wondrous fumbling in which they were so desperate to take something, anything, uncertain of just what they were holding in their hands. Now they knew how precious the love they had between them was, and they explored it like an appraiser studying a fine jewel, growing more and more excited as they realized what a treasure they truly had in each other. This was a once-in-a-lifetime find. This love was a world-building love. A foundation block in a castle where happily-ever-after lived. He could feel it in her kiss.

The knowledge thrilled through him as their skin finally touched with no barriers to hold them back. It was just skin-on-skin in freshly laundered sheets. The fan hummed somewhere beyond them as Sahana straddled him, her knees pinned to either side of his legs. The world beyond him blurred as she leaned in, all hot skin and slight smile, moving across his body like a breeze. It was too hot out there, and she was his only breath of fresh air, giggling as he nipped at her neck, laugh melting into a gasp as he spread her legs a little further apart and took what he wanted, what he'd been dreaming of for so long. She urged him on, nails trailing across his shoulders, digging into his back. Her arms enveloped him in a tight grasp as their bodies moved together in a perfect wave of motion.

He could hardly breathe, could barely see, eyes blurry and out of focus. It was like standing too close to an impressionistic painting, knowing that everything in your field of vision was an important and lovely detail, but unable to see the full picture. He took her in in breaths, in moments. Maybe later he'd be able to string her into a poem, but for now, he was just living her. Everything around him was Sahana, the faint hint of her perfume still sticking to her skin and the thin sheen of sweat she'd worked up moving against him. She made such wonderful sounds, better than any music he'd ever heard, and he relished in pulling the noises from her, fingers trailing her body until he heard her breathing hitch, then bringing his mouth to the space his hands vacated and scraping his teeth over them. She'd gasp and moan, writhing on top of him, urging him to do more, to feel more, to take more of her.

With her in his hands, he felt like an artist, working with a new material, untamed and wild, not quite perfect, not seamless, but wonderful nonetheless. Maybe they'd end up messy on top of each other. Maybe his hands would be forever stained from loving her, unable to touch another woman without remembering where they'd been. But he couldn't imagine ever touching another woman.

No one would be as responsive or as free with him, as full of love as she trailed worshipful kisses down his chest. With no other person would he ever be so perfectly in sync, their very breaths flowing together, their hearts beating to the exact same rhythm. Sex was supposed to be more awkward than this, wasn't it? With elbows and knees going places they shouldn't, cramping fingers and sides and strange noises. But if she had to steady herself on his shoulders to stay upright and if he made a sound in the back of his throat that made them both dissolve into helpless laughter, he was all the happier to feel her breath on his neck and let her pull him closer.

Eventually, she'd tighten up and gasp in such a way that his heart would nearly stop. She'd collapse and roll away from him, gasping as she came back into her body, smiling a thick, sated smile at him as she reached up for another kiss, softer this time. When the passion ebbed, pure love was what that remained. He felt it in his soul as he lost himself in one more kiss.

Twenty-Four

Eight Months Later

Solitude. Even with his soul hemmed neatly into another's, the way his was to Sahana's, there were still moments like these. Moments in which he could settle into his couch and breathe easily as the world continued its forward motion without having to worry about what others thought. That was one of the best gifts Sahana could give him, far more precious than any cufflink or a bottle of rare scotch. The time and space to be himself, to be Vikram. That is: to write.

His only companion was his notebook, once blank pages and an uncracked spine, now stuffed with words. It had been another loving gift from Sahana with the words, *"Poet, Write,"* emblazoned in her graceful hand on its dedication page. Now, just as she'd commanded, it was brimming with words, so many poems, and long rambling rewrites.

He never lacked imagination these days. With Sahana in his home, it felt as though the world was at his feet. With life conquered and everything else enveloped in the rosy haze of happily ever after, there was still something to write about. And it was always something good. He wouldn't be the writer he was now if he hadn't had Sahana's love supporting him, her hand in his hand, her lips pressing a kiss at his temple.

Vikram had once believed that true poetry, the best verse ever written, could only have been sparked from pain, from loss. In the lives of poets there always seemed to be so much pain. So many dark days. But now he knew that all those dark moments shaped the verses of those poets, and in the sweet days of their lives, glowing golden and peppered with kisses, in that ease, real writing could begin.

Vikram had already lived through dark days. And every bitter memory made the brush of Sahana's mouth against his all the sweeter. Holding her in his arms, he was always drawn to the present moment, always caught up in the joy of her breath against his neck, her laughter in his ear. Because letting his mind drift towards the shadows of the past seemed a useless pursuit when he had Sahana, shining like the sun, before him. His future was blindingly bright.

Sometimes things were so lovely he put the pen aside and took her into his arms. Vikram had never been much of a dancer, a little shyer than most of his friends in that regard, but with Sahana in his arms, he couldn't help but love showing her off on a dancefloor, for jealous and admiring eyes to see. She was all his. And the way she looked up at him, her eyes full of all the love her heart felt, it made his pulse race with the thought of their future. He could see them dancing together on their wedding day.

It was pretty little glimpses of the future that kept them moving forward. On days when work frustrated them or bad news on the television cast the whole world in a bleak, sick light, they could find solace in each other. And on days when even love wasn't enough, they could each turn to a book, lying on the couch with their legs tangled and their minds far away, able to grace each other with the escape that fantasy provided until they were ready to face life once more.

Life worked because they made it work. Love like this wouldn't have worked with anyone besides Sahana, because no one shared his soul the way she did. She understood things about him that he hadn't even noticed, and the language both their souls spoke was one that induced such ease in their lives. They lived in harmony that many people spent their whole marriages striving for, because their similarities allowed them to look at each other, as though in a mirror, and care for one another with that deep, clear insight. She understood the muses that ruled his life – silence, good food, the written word. And they pursued those muses together.

Over the past few months, so many hard things in Vikram's life had softened. He hadn't even realized the discomfort that had filled his previous life existed until Sahana took them away. Instead of microwave roti and quiet nights alone with a book, they'd go to the cyber hub with Nalini and her husband, or spend an evening with a glass of wine on the porch of a new restaurant, tasting what the city had to offer in the glimmering lights and arguing about whose hometown cooked better.

"This meal was incredible, but in the end, there's no food on this earth like New Delhi food," she insisted once their plates were cleared and they shared a dessert of rice pudding, two spoons in one bowl. It was a welcome cool treat in the midst of such an oppressive summer heatwave. "There's no food like the food they make five kilometers from here," he countered, feeding her a bite and smiling as her eyes closed in pure bliss, "and another five kilometers over? A completely different dining experience. There's no culinary life like the Indian culinary life."

She drank to that and touched their wine glasses together. He signed the check and carried her bag to the car because she was a little tipsy and just wanted to hold his hand. Under all the stars and city lights, she shone just as bright as any of them, contesting any celestial body to gleam quite the way she could whenever she looked at him.

Vikram could only stare back because that was his life now: blindingly brilliant. Even at work he seemed to glow and his friends had all noticed. He wondered how he'd ever been ashamed to show his face when now he had a lipstick mark from Sahana to wipe off his cheek each morning as he made his way to the sales floor. He wanted everyone to see that he was a man in love. That he loved Sahana, and she loved him back.

Here, in the very place where so many of their troubles began, sprung from a poisoned seed and blooming into such a dangerous rumor, he wanted to make sure those rumors didn't live in the light of day. That everyone who knew them understood that there was nothing sordid or unsavory to them, but that they were growing each day in love and respect for each other. He was vigilant about any darkness that might have lingered after Ashok's transgressions. He'd fight it away. For Sahana's sake as well as his own. They deserved some rest, some peace, a life free of the pain Ashok had tried to cause.

It seemed as though everyone in the office wanted the same thing. Certainly Mr. Patil did, and Nalini as well. Everyone else fell in sync behind them. They all felt the warmth and were drawn towards their relationship like moths to a flame. Vikram had never been popular, he'd been tolerated and pitied a little and sometimes hated when the sales team had a deadline towards which he had to drive them. But with Sahana by his side, his happiness must have softened him or shaped him into a more likeable man. Now that he was a we, "we" were well-liked indeed.

He hoped he wouldn't see the end until they were old and gray. He couldn't envision his future without her now. He couldn't imagine falling asleep without the sound of her breath, without his lips in her hair as she rested against his chest, secure in whatever dream she was living and knowing that she'd awake to something greater than even her imagination could conceive. That was what love was-- it made dreaming useless. Vikram used to spend his nights dreaming of a life that wasn't his, thinking it could never be true, that happiness was for other people, and rest was a concept that only book characters could achieve once their stories were over. Now he knew for a fact that all the things he'd dreamed about could be true. He held that truth in his hands every time Sahana rolled over in bed, blinking away the cobwebs of sleep, stretching out her muscles before she yawned and said, "Good morning, my love."

Just like she had this morning. She'd rolled over to look in his eyes, and must have seen the thoughts swimming behind them, because she smiled a smile that showed she knew things about him that he was still learning about himself. She slipped out of bed before he could kiss her properly and dressed. Looking back at him over her shoulder as she slipped on her blouse, she said, "I'll go out to pick up breakfast today. Why don't you stay in and write?"

It was a lazy Sunday morning, the sort that was perfect for sleeping through. But he'd woken before she had, stirred by his own thoughts. He'd watched the rise and fall of her chest for a bit before the rhythm of her breath lulled him into a nearly meditative state, and he lost himself in thoughts of love and the future. He'd once thought that dreamers could never truly be happy. Now he knew they could be happy, but they might still stay lost.

The only way out was the notebook. It was the place where he could organize his thoughts and turn them into whatever verse he'd like to read at the open mic on Monday. So, he flipped it to the nearest blank page and traced a map of their lives together, watching them cross from one season to the next together, hand in hand. Each moment became a stanza, and each stanza got brighter and brighter. As he composed, he watched them moving out of the darkness and into the light.

It took him hours. Sahana returned at some point. He wasn't sure how long she stood in the doorway, watching him write. She didn't say anything, and he hadn't even heard the key turning in the lock. (He'd given her a key only a couple weeks after they started dating. She'd fallen into living in his apartment without either of them noticing. She was still paying the lease on her apartment, but only because it would cost more to break her lease). At some point she'd grown tired of standing and dropped a kiss on his head as she passed him, pausing only to set a travel cup of coffee on his side table. He reached up and caught her hand, pulling her in for a deeper kiss. "That was lovely," she whispered, before kissing his ear once more and retiring to the bedroom to finish the novel she'd been devouring.

The coffee was cold by the time Vikram was ready to show Sahana the poem he had finished. Even after he finally pulled his pen from the page, he blushed a little, reading over the lines. Each one meant so much to him. Each one was carefully crafted to show Sahana what he felt, what he was thinking, just how much he cared. He knew that if he didn't show it to her soon, he'd scrap the whole thing in embarrassment and hide it away. But he couldn't show up to the open mic empty-handed, and he couldn't write some trite piece of nothing with no emotional meaning anymore. Every page he wrote was filled with his thoughts about Sahana. This was just the page he was willing to share.

When he peeked into his room, he saw Sahana propped up on her elbows, eyes scanning the pages of a paperback novel. That almost sent him back towards his notebook, trying to capture that moment before it disappeared. But this was their future. There would be a million more moments just like it. So, he stepped forward and said, "Here, I have something for you to read."

She smiled and dropped her book. She began to read aloud.

Our Every Kiss is a Poem
Vikram Shan

You dwelled once in the depths of despair.
on the floor of the sea you lay drowning.
My voice, water-distorted, reached your ear.

Through the roiling of the sea,
you learned to swim and swam to me
chased the sun until water turned to breeze

a dry world sparkling with dew
that took its first breath that day--
(but you'd know all about that.)

After all, you were the oxygen
electric glimmer of living water
spritely bubbling in the lungs

of a creature sleeping, dreaming
stuck in heavy-limbed hypnosis
trapped in the amber sap of time.

(me, before you.
how lucky that you
never knew him.)

When I first woke bathed in your glow,
I thought to thrash away the radiance,

afraid of light after life with eyes closed,

But you blanketed me in your warmth.
A summer's day in soothing heat,
melting the numbing ice that held me

Then I knew you were a light to guide
And not a spark to scar my skin again.
(I remembered what it was to burn.)

Now I am your soldier. I follow you.
When I march to the beat of your life,
Our footsteps fall in perfect sync.

I am a poet.
I know what it is to walk
A metered line.

And when I fall out of time
It is the press of your lips that brings me
Right back to the start.

For a moment, she was silent. Vikram scanned the poem in his mind to see if he'd written something to offend her, something to stun her into such silence. But he could find nothing. Finally, she looked up at him, that smile playing across her face. "It's good," she said. "Let's write another one."

"Another poem?" he asked blankly, and she took his wrist, laughing, as she pulled him closer.

"Another poem," she agreed, and kissed him. "Here, let me show you how."